GW00359310

CRANNÓG 49 autu

ISSN 1649-4865
ISBN 978-1-907017-52-0

Cover image: 'Telling Lies', encaustic and oil, by Ann-Marie Brown
Cover image sourced by Sandra Bunting
Cover design by Wordsonthestreet
Published by Wordsonthestreet for Crannóg magazine
www.wordsonthestreet.com @wordsstreet

CONTENTS

Submissions for Crannóg 50 open November 1st until November 30th
Publication date is February 22nd 2019

Crannóg is published three times a year in spring, summer and autumn.

Submission Times: Month of November for spring issue. Month of March for summer issue. Month of July for autumn issue.

We will <u>not read</u> submissions sent outside these times.

POETRY: Send no more than three poems. Each poem should be under 50 lines.

PROSE: Send one story. Stories should be under 2,000 words.

We do not accept postal submissions.

When emailing your submission we require **three** *things:*

1. *The text of your submission included both in body of email and as a Word attachment (this is to ensure correct layout. We may, however, change your layout to suit our publication).*
2. *A brief bio in the third person. Include this both in body and in attachment.*
3. *A postal address for contributor's copy in the event of publication.*

For full submission details, to learn more about Crannóg Magazine, to purchase copies of the current issue, or take out a subscription, log on to our website:

www.crannogmagazine.com

THE SKIN OF EARTH   UNA MANNION

M y brother Michael was born with a caul. When he was handed to my mother, a translucent veil of skin covered his head and face. She said it shimmered. She was told how it was lucky, that she should save it. She kept it in the top drawer of her dresser with our birth certificates and old photographs. Sometimes when she was out at work, we opened the drawer, carefully parting the tissue paper to reveal the shrivelled piece of membrane inside. We were both repelled and drawn to his talisman. We threatened to steal it, to throw away his magic, but we never dared disturb it. We draped our faces with wet washcloths to tease him.

'You were born without a face.'

Mrs Wolff said there was magic on that boy. After our father died, she'd come to stay with us while our mother worked. She walked with a stick and sucked hard butterscotch sweets that she kept in the front pocket of her house dress. She had cat-eye glasses and a flattened bouffant. Most days she watched us from the sofa smoking Kent menthols. There were seven of us and the older ones chased after the little ones. Mrs Wolff could barely walk; it took her a long time to get up from the couch, and she didn't like to hurry. Old age had dried her skin and it was itchy. She rolled down her support hose and we sat at her feet scratching her shins for her, listening to her tell stories.

Michael tormented her. He'd disappear out of his bed in the night and then ring the front doorbell. She'd make all that effort to get to the front door and answer it and he would be standing out there in the dark in his pyjamas. If Mrs Wolff knew about the laundry chute in the bedroom closet, she never said.

'That Michael,' she'd chuckle, 'he's something else.' She had a heart condition which made her breathing heavy and her ankles wide like elephant legs. 'You'll kill me one of these days,' she'd scold, and then reward him with a butterscotch.

Michael charmed adults, shouldered payphones and money fell out, kicked vending machines and Twinkies offered themselves. Once we dug for treasure in the woods behind the High School and he unburied a twenty-dollar bill. I believed he might be magic.

When the plumber came to our basement to find a burst pipe underneath the cement foundation, we all went down to watch him. Mrs Wolff had told us that he was like a wizard and could divine water. He considered the seven of us lined up.

'Show me your hands,' he said. We all held our arms out. He hovered his hand above our outstretched ones and lingered when he came to Michael's. Michael's fingernail tips were slivers of black moons. We'd been building dirt tracks, bridges and jumps for his matchbox cars. He took Michael's small hand in his big ones and held it, passing his palm across it.

'You,' he said, and he handed Michael a tree limb that forked into two branches.

'That's just a tree,' said Thomas. He was the eldest and Mrs Wolff said he was like the biblical Thomas, always doubting.

'It's a hazel rod,' said the plumber. 'Just let them pull you,' he said to Michael. 'Hold them like this.' Michael gripped the two ends of the branch and carried it with arms straight out, elbows hardly bent, as if he were riding an invisible bicycle with wooden handles. He moved across the grey concrete of the basement. He started towards the right, then circled slowly as if drawn towards the corner where we kept the wellies and winter boots. He stopped. The tip of the rod strained and bent towards the ground.

'You're doing that, Michael,' I said, disbelieving.

'Did he find it? Is that it?' asked Thomas.

The plumber knelt, pressing the side of his face against the ground.

'Shhhh,' he said. We all held our breath while he listened to the earth. He stood up, brushed down his trousers and patted Michael on the back.

'Well done. That's the leak.'

I believed Michael really could see into the ground. Mrs Wolff said there was only a thin veil of earth between us and our ancestors below and that Michael was closer to them than most. I wondered if that included our father. Since he'd died, I tagged behind Michael, carrying sandwich bags of creek water crowded with tadpoles he'd caught, or served as his torch-bearer with a jar of fireflies tied to the end of a stick to light his path. I set up tin cans on stumps so he could target practice in the woods with a BB gun he'd secretly bought from one of the Natale brothers.

In sixth grade, things changed. Michael started getting into trouble, failing tests, and horsing around with the wrong crowd. Thomas said he was haunted like the boy in *The Shining* who was also born with a caul. Mrs Wolff told me to stop worrying, he wasn't possessed, that his clowning was a powerful weapon. She finished with us that year and moved back to her trailer with her two pugs. My mother worked nights and Michael got worse. He ignored her calls to get ready in the mornings and made us late for school, rolling down the stairs from his bedroom still in his sleeping bag, making us laugh, already dressed in our uniforms, schoolbags in hand. Even when she cradled his head in the crook of her arm and banged it off the wall, he didn't cry. We stood on the steps whispering, 'Please stop.' When she did, she looked as bewildered as us, his head in her arms.

She said she couldn't manage him. I blamed what happened with Greg. Greg was my mom's car mechanic and new boyfriend. He wore a shirt with his name stitched on it with the sleeves cut off. He drove a red Chevy pickup truck with beer cans thrown on the back bed. One night we had all climbed on to the truck. It was dark and when Greg came out Michael said something Greg didn't like and Greg said he was going to teach that boy a lesson in manners and went for him. We knew he meant it. One of us had dropped the tailgate and Greg ran into it and cursed and flailed in the dark. We all scattered; Michael went for the woods. I knew he was probably running down the trail, something he could do in pitch black and Greg would never catch him. Bridget and I crouched beneath the azaleas. Greg was shouting about us goddamn brats and my mother was screaming that she was calling the police and for him to leave and never come back. Greg went to go, but sped up and down our driveway first, accelerating forward, braking hard, then reversing at speed and screeching to a stop, burning rubber in the dark.

She sent Michael to Branch Creek Farm School. He didn't want to go. It was a boarding school for boys from one-parent homes like ours.

9

They were woken before dawn to do their farm chores. Michael's job was to look after pigs that were turned into scrapple, bacon and sausages sold in a shop at the side of the road. When we read the story of the prodigal son among the swine at school, I imagined my own brother amongst the pigs, their breath and his exhaling ghost shapes in the dark frosty morning. Michael was only twelve, and I wondered what gifts he'd squandered to bring him to such exile.

A few months after he'd left, I came home from school and Mrs Wolff's Oldsmobile was parked outside. I could smell her in our house, her cigarettes, talcum powder, the Jerkins cream she rubbed on her dry legs. The kitchen door was shut and she and my mother were talking in low voices. I knew something was wrong. I sat on the bottom of the stairs and listened. A teacher at Branch Creek had been fired for hurting boys. He was also Michael's house-parent. Michael had called Mrs Wolf collect from a payphone and said he wanted to come home. My mother said the school had informed her of everything that had happened, that she was happy with how they had handled it. She'd spoken to Michael and he'd said nothing happened to him. She said he was better off there.

'I can't manage him. It's hard enough as it is with all of them.'

'He can come live with me,' said Mrs Wolff.

'In your trailer with the dogs? No.'

'He's a child who's lost his father.'

'I know you mean well, but stop interfering.'

My mother sounded like she did when she spoke to the electric company about an overdue bill. Mrs Wolff opened the kitchen door and walked right past me on the steps as if she didn't see me. I watched her from the living room window walk towards her car. It was late autumn and she used her stick to push leaves off the sidewalk, the bare tree limbs across the road reached with gnarled arms towards the sky. I went upstairs to Michael's room, crawled into his sleeping bag and pulled it over my head.

I started writing him letters, telling him everything and nothing, trying to reel him back towards us because already I could feel him spinning away. Danny Kriegan was caught stealing beer. Kelly Smith had a boyfriend who was 18 and her fourteenth birthday was still weeks away. 'We miss you,' I signed. Michael's letters said very little. The pigs weren't so bad. He'd been in a fight. He wrote on Branch Creek postcards that advertised their own bacon.

At Christmas, we went to Michael's school pageant. It was snowing when we arrived and boys dressed in robes and crowns ran past us in twos and threes towards the chapel. Street lights cast golden circles on the snow. I searched among the robed boys but couldn't find him. Inside the small chapel, Christmas trees, small fairy lights and velvet red ribbons decorated the altar. Green pine garlands were woven around the pews, pulpit and rails. The church bells rang, the organ started and the sound of voices singing drew towards us as the schoolboys processed up the aisle.

The choir came first, the boys in deep red robes with white surplices followed by the cast, striding down the aisle bearing their gifts. My mother and the rest of us in our dresses and suits craned our necks to see Michael. Finally, I saw him when he and another boy came forward to light candles. I nudged Bridget next to me. I decided when I saw him, I would tease him about wearing a dress. But outside the chapel afterwards, I couldn't remember any of the insults or stories I had saved up to tell him and didn't feel like teasing him anymore.

'You're like an altar boy,' was all I said.

'Hey farm boy, are you a swine expert now?' Thomas said. Michael shrugged and looked away.

Thomas looked wounded. 'I'm just kidding,' he said.

Michael didn't say anything, just lifted one of his shoulders and let it drop. The snow was still falling in thick flakes. We talked awkwardly, like we didn't know what to say to him, as if we hardly knew each other. Michael answered in mumbled monosyllables. My mother said we needed to get going, the roads were going to be treacherous.

Some of us tried to hug Michael, but he kept his arms stiff at his side, his shoulders hunched under the surplice. We left him on the side of the hill outside the chapel, and walked towards the parking lot, passing boys still in their costumes, crowns on their heads in small circles of family. One of the little ones started crying and

11

Thomas told her to shut up, then picked her up and held her. I wished we hadn't come. I wished we had never come.

At the car, we stood while my mother searched for the keys. Everything was quiet in that hush snow brings and the stillness of farmland at night. I heard the jingle of the found keys as something hit the back of my head. A shock of cold ran down my back. I looked behind me towards the chapel and saw Michael on the ground, scooping up snow. Other robed figures flapped down to join him, packing snow to pelt the departing families. Thomas and I hurtled back towards them. Michael reached me first, tackling me and rubbing my face in the snow, whooping. I was laughing so hard I couldn't get up. Michael left me. Face down in a drift, I could hear all the shouts and laughter above me as if far away in the distance, above the quiet ground where I was cocooned. I wanted to stay there, to hold back time and everything painful ahead of us. I rolled over and lay there on my back looking up at the sky as icy water ran down my cheeks and neck. The streetlights lit the falling snow, the flakes like falling stars, and all around me the skin of the earth shimmered.

ARTHUR POWER'S 'CONNEMARA TROUT' LIAM AUNGIER

(In the National Gallery of Ireland, Dublin)

A stone the builders had rejected:
Galway marble, as green as the sea
And bubbled, faulted with imperfections,

Before it fell under his grey eye,
His coarse hands working their miracle:
Prising from rock a brace of sea-trout.

Open-mouthed, wide-eyed, I might
Mistake one for that salmon in the Boyne
Elusive, fabled, slippery

With knowledge. I could believe them
The two small fishes of the Gospels
That fed the multitude.

13

A GALLERY OF MEMORIES   CHINUA EZENWA-OHAETO

My Grandmother was a gallery of memories and
a display of things like flowers growing out from graves.
Once she said: *here, to give birth is pain. not to give birth is pain.*
Maybe that is why every mark on our backs is a lens into our inside.
Before she left, her mouth was full of places and maps;
she could tell how, why and when towns came about:
the junctions and supermarkets and offices, the churches and
mosques ...
Somewhere inside of her is a well of houses and lineages,
each is marked by the name of the owner of the owner of the owner.
I think she was a hard drive. I think she was a map without a map.
When sending out greetings, she placed a yam in my hand
and drew the routes and corners to a house in my ears.
I wondered how such an old, indoors for six years and more,
could know places, despite the new sprouts and billboards.
My friend said that Grandmothers are spirits, they know things,
they feel things, they understand things, and they go places in one
place.
My Grandmother was a gallery of memories and
a display of things like flowers growing out from graves.

BÁS BEATHA PANTOUM AMANDA BELL

'Bás Beatha – Survival in a Nuclear War'*
said to build a refuge room and wait,
for the safety of the home and farm:
you've never seen the stars, or rain.

Build a refuge room and wait,
then sweep the fallout off the roofs:
you've never seen the stars, or rain,
shut in a windowless ward, indoors.

The fallout didn't coat the roofs
but swept like dust across the sky
shutting you in a ward, indoors,
in fear of every drop and mite.

It swept like dust across the sky;
meat was burned and milk poured out
in fear of every drop and mite –
not a thing remained untouched.

Meat was burned and milk poured out,
for safety on the home and farm.
Not a thing remains untouched:
survival, in a nuclear war.

Irish Civil Defence booklet, published 1965

15

THE INNOCENT COSMOPOLITAN   EMILY CULLEN

If I imagine I'm Dorothy Parker
expel smoke slowly from a cigarette holder
in a silken kimono on a languid afternoon,
conjure my wit while pounding keys,
a brandy and lime within easy reach.

If I feign I am Lauren Bacall,
unamused by the jejune, gesture
through an alluring smokescreen,
arch a piqued brow as I smoulder
demurely at Humphrey Bogart.

If I channel Coco Chanel,
loll in shimmering sweeps of pearls,
behind a fanlike spray of fronds
will I get beyond girlish feelings
to that swagger I secretly long for?

Am I palsied by the claim
I'm 'innocently cosmopolitan',
the taunt of an old flame?
Fine, if one can fairly say, I'll be
at the apogee of suavity one day.

ALL THROUGH THE NIGHT ANGELA GRAHAM

I look back now with a kind of dread, yet dread is about the future, about what's going to happen, not what has already happened. So I dread ...? The memory of pain.

I never thought of myself as a man given to gestures. Imagination I do have, but I tend to keep it to myself.

I remember the road; the little road under the starlight that summer. It was the year Mam and Dad sold the farm. I didn't want it. They kept the farmhouse and the little *bwthyn* that had been the kernel of the homestead. You and I had used it for years already for holidays with the kids. They loved its thick walls and deep window-ledges.

At *Clogwyn Uchel*, on the very edge of Wales, the roads are dark (some of them are tracks, really) and the stars sort of spread themselves out overhead, display themselves, with a careless glamour; or like something much more homely, like sugar spilt across a slate, but up there, up above. A sprinkling of sugar overhead. Very confusing if you thought about it too much. And higher into the sky – it's hard to describe! – there's a hazy cloud of them. Growing up at *Clogwyn Uchel* and I never bothered to learn much about them. Anyway, the stars do what they do whether we notice them or not. They're not waiting for our attention.

On a clear night like that one they shed enough light to see your way and the chalky ground of the lane helps. It's a glimmering path up to the *bwthyn*, reflecting light from far, far above. Sometimes it even seems to me as though a bit of the sky has dropped to earth because the little white stones are like a rough and tumble Milky Way between the hedges.

You walked ahead of me, Mari. Blindly, I thought. Or like someone who'd been dazzled by something. Your feet took you.

Your mind? Numbed.

Probably. We all have to do so much guess-work about each other! What is she feeling? What will she do next? What does she want?

'Do you love him?' I called out. But you didn't stop, or look back, or speak. I'm sure you heard me. You went on, into the little house.

I couldn't. I walked around it to where the sea suddenly presents itself. A shock! Always. Always that shiver at finding yourself on the edge of a cliff. Acres of water ahead in a dark mass. The endlessness of the sea. It doesn't stop. It goes about its business, rushing and crushing, floating boats, flexing itself. That night it was shuddering.

The stars. Some flung themselves down the sky. Mad bastards. Most looked on in a dignified way, blinking mildly at this recklessness. And I thought of the song. Its beautiful tune.

Holl amrantau'r sêr ddywedant
Ar hyd y nos.

Ar hyd y nos. All through the night.

Nothing like the crappy English version. Sickly-sweet, that. And boring. 'Soft the drowsy hours are creeping ... visions of delight revealing ... hill and vale in slumber steeping'. And the stars don't get a look-in! Not a mention. You pointed that out to me. When you were learning Welsh. 'How come ...?' you asked. You were always asking that. 'Why is the verb here? Why do I have to say ...?' Whatever.

And I'd say, 'It just is, Mari. I don't know why. Ask your teacher, *cariad*. Gwyn knows all that stuff.'

Yes, he did, didn't he? *Holl amrantau'r sêr* ... *amrantau* – such a great-sounding word for such a workaday bit of us; our eyelids. 'All the eyelids of the stars are saying'. Eyelids speak? Oh, yes. They shield or conceal. They widen to reveal.

Dyma'r ffordd i fro gogoniant.
'This is the way to the land of glory. All through the night.'

Go on, stars, I remember thinking that night, as I stood with them all above me, show us the way.

Oh, I closed my eyes then, I did. Because I was lost.

That stuff from the bible swam into my head:

Pan edrychwyf ar y nefoedd, gwaith dy fysedd...

'When I consider thy heavens, the work of thy fingers ...' How does it go? 'The stars which thou hast ordained ... What is man, that thou art mindful of him? ... a little lower than the angels ... crowned with glory and honour ...'

Shit. Nothing like a chapel upbringing for loading you with stuff that makes you feel like shit in comparison. Sunday school set pieces. So beautiful the pictures in your head. No special effects needed. Just the words. You can see it happening: the stars being set in place one by one, like diamonds. And look at them up there, murmuring cheerfully to one another, 'Here we are! Just where we should be. But we'll cast ourselves from heaven in an instant. Give the word. No problem.'

But me? I was bloody lost. Lost.

We'd gone walking on the beach, earlier, you and me, between the pebbly border of the sea and the wrack and old bits of driftwood and plastic oddments that stack up high against the cliff. Between that stony fringe – it always hurt my feet as a child; I'd teeter across it, complaining, excited at my own bravery, me versus the chilly little waves; like someone walking over hot coals, I'd think, secretly proud (look at me, Mam! Dad!) – between those stones and the cliff there's a narrow crescent of smooth beige sand. It doesn't change. Same for our kids as it had been for me. You and I walked along it towards the setting sun but you wouldn't look at me and couldn't speak. Couldn't, I say, because you just shook your head sadly at every question.

We ended up just walking. I found myself scrutinising the sun's angle – how the low shafts of sun hit the beach – and how they struck stars out of the damp sand: tiny mica fragments that glinted ahead of every step I took. Walking on a constellation. Yes, I could think a thought like that even with all that was going on because that's the kind of mind I've got. I don't like misery. I sheer off it. Think of something else! Cheer up! It'll never happen.

But that night? Not a single bloody joke.

So later, when I stood out there in the darkness in front of the *bwthyn*, I looked up at the stars and I thought: we're surrounded; we haven't a chance. Stars above us. Stars below us. And we're stuck in the middle. The shit in the sandwich. Who'd want to stay here? Why would you stay?

And then, I knew you were behind me. I felt you. You were still inside, mind; behind me, looking out through the window of the dark house; looking out at the same pointlessly lovely display, the Plough and all the other things we don't know the names of, you and me.

And I was desperate and I suppose it was so I wouldn't cry that I did it. I started to sing. Was I showing you I didn't care? Big man. Mad man to *sing* at a time like that!

Golau arall yw tywyllwch,

I arddangos gwir brydferthwch,

'Darkness is another type of light' – to show us true beauty, the beauty of 'the family of the heavens', the stars, 'in silence, all through the night'.

And I went on, louder; that tune rising, like a wave rolling up to its crest,

Nos yw henaint pan ddaw cystudd

'Night is old age'. That's 'when trouble hits us'; really hits us. Hits us when we're least able for it; gets us in an armlock and grinds us down, Mam and Dad.

And the tune sinks gradually, gradually, into calm and quiet, like a wave relaxing. Dark night is coming, it tells us; our youth is dead. I couldn't roll with the blows so well. I was getting the measure of myself a bit, frankly: a man in my middle years; nothing special.

Ond i harddu dyn a'i hwyrddydd

'But to make ourselves and our day's end beautiful ...' – to have something (at least something) to hold on to – 'let's put our fragile lights together ... All through the night'.

I couldn't help it. I couldn't, couldn't help it. I just cried.

I'd thought you'd always be there, see. *Ar hyd y nos.*

I stood out there and I cried. And I knew you were watching me. And I couldn't stop.

Pity, was it, that made you stay that night? The next morning the sky was like the inside of a sea shell, pearly pink and white. The stars had gone. We were still there.

Later, much later, you told me that when you'd looked out you'd thought, *My husband, singing in the darkness.* I had surprised you. You saw me silhouetted against the sky while a star dropped gracefully across it, beyond me, and you thought: *Have I just watched the last moment of something that's millions of years old?* You saw, you told me – as though it were really there – the white heart of a November bonfire, the children's figures scampering, black, against it; bunches of sparks dancing up above the orange flames; and one particular spark, floating, higher and higher, wavering, till it expired, gently, and as silently as a shooting star.

And, there I was, one particular man. As though I'd come into focus again. And you chose. Because however hard things had become we had created a life together. Something real. Something real as a mad bastard singing on a cliff-top. You chose me. Just for tonight, you told me you remembered thinking: we'll see about tomorrow.

Our fragile lights. Together. We do what we can. Our lives are brief and *Hir yw'r nos.* Night is long.

And so, today, I've chosen: your name, with stars above and stars below. We walk on stars, with stars high overhead but life is in the middle, *pan ddaw cystudd, cariad.* A rough road, my love.

The mason's asked me why I have him carving stars on your stone. I'll tell him, but everyone else, as time goes by, will have to work it out for themselves.

21

OUR SECRET   KIM WHYSALL-HAMMOND

Take the third turn over there
by the weeping willow at the barren stream.
Turn sharp now into brightness
or you will miss the crease,
that flaw in time's weave you must push through
(sometimes my shoulder gets stuck, but I persevere).
Once through, stay low, part and peer through high grasses
watch the herds roll past.
Tusks upraised, immense cinnamon woolly hulks,
regally righteous, grassland behemoths,
lords of the plains
(yes, indeed, the land is flatter here that it was back now).
Be ready for the noise when they cry out,
it reverberates all through your bones
oscillating ears to numbness.
The hulk and bulk of them is prodigious
and worth the squeeze.
Whether it is worth the panic
when you finally realise
the directions home are missing?

Is up to you.

VOYAGERS   THEODORE DEPPE

Trinidad Head, California. i.m. Dermot Healy

Rather than peer through blurred lenses,
I tuck my glasses into the raincoat's pocket
and the drops on my hood sound like the play of rain
on a tent when it's possible to sleep late.
Base notes of surf below as I climb the headland,

and the sprung rhythm of the bell buoys,
mad with spondees. Sea lions call, riding those buoys,
and from the ferns, glistening near the abyss,
the song of a wren. I watch the crumpled Pacific, hoping
for a glimpse of gray whales heading north,

but if they are out there they pass unseen,
letting fog horns take their place. I try to respond
by imitating Mongolian throat singing, rolling
a low *oooooo*-sound around my tongue,
but can't find that harmonic overtone

that the writer Dermot Healy once tried to teach me
in a pub in Letterkenny, a sound as much of a prayer
as a growl though his gift frightened some patrons.
Years later, his body was removed from the wake house
in Maugherow to a farewell of throat music.

I go down into my chest and try to send
paired tones out across the water when a hiker
with unruly hair rounds the path and catches me
mid-song. Rather than avert his eyes or laugh
he beams at me, roars, 'Good man!'

then lumbers off. O brother, for a moment
I thought I recognized you. What distances
did you travel to come here this morning?
Where are you headed
with your red rucksack and crushed smile?

CARTOGRAPHY OF MEMORY   KARLA VAN VLIET

The tall black locust trees are flowering.
I am walking in the night, so I don't realize
the white clustered blossoms have opened
until scent fills the dim lamp-lit street under
this new moon sky and I breathe in an ocean.
I've always thought this is what love smells like.
It's no surprise that it is late and I am walking
and you are hovering like memory and distance.
The white florets smell of you. Smell of crumpled
sheets and light entering slant through the window.
Smell of your fingers tracing the mountain rise
of my hip, the warmth of your breath on my skin.
Our youth, so beautiful and full of possibility.
We can't go back and change the maps we followed
away from that afternoon. There is only where we are.
Territories we have conquered in our own small ways,
and borders we dare not cross. Oh, the unknown
waters, where dragons dwell.

LULL   COLIN BANCROFT

We walked from the car park, past restaurants
And souvenir shops closed for the winter.
The cold plumes of our breath seemed to haunt
The path that sheared off the cliff in splinters

Of rough cut stone dropping down to the beach.
The track gave way to a bubble-wrap of shells
And we turned rocks for crabs left by the breach
Of the retreating waves and pooling swells.

The foreshore stretched far, waterlogged, a lawn
Left to seed but undone by a shower of rain.
Far out on the horizon, like some dark dawn,
The sea's massed ranks started to come again.

MY SPELLING SENTENCES WEEK: 6 BY: LUCY AGE 7 ½
SEÁN KENNY

'tr' words: trot, tram, treat, trek, trip
1. A frog does not **trot**, but ponys do. In My Litl Pony, the ponys trot around! (My favrit pony is Twilight sparkle – she is a magic unicorn!!!)
2. The Luas is a **tram** that you get into town and i like when it goes bing bing bing but not when drunk peple come on it.
3. My uncl brings me a lot of **treat**s like choclat and Haribo and sumtimes extra secret ones that my mam does not see that I hide in my room in a speshal place in my wardrobe.
4. Me and my mam always have to **trek** to Lidl because my dad needs the car for stuff.
5. When i am in bed sometimes I hear my dad **trip** wen he comes in.

'gr' words: grip, grab, grin, gram, grow

1. I have a pencil **grip** it is purple, and that is my favrit colur!!
2. My uncl always **grab**s me wen he comes to my house and I tell him stop but sometimes it tickles and makes me laff and he does not stop.
3. A **grin** is a smile. My mam grins wen she takes selfies and puts them on Facebook but she does not grin a lot.
4. **Gram**s is for the amownt of something you put in a cake like 300 grams of flower. Sometimes wen my dad is on the fone he says how many grams?
5. Wen I **grow** up i want to be a vet or maybe a astronaut. (But i realy realy want to be a unicorn vet!!!)

'dr' words: drum, dress, drop, drag, dream

1. I do not like loud noises like a **drum** or shouting or things hitting off the wall.
2. My mam has a foto in her weding **dress** and i realy like this foto becaus she looks happy in the foto.

3. My dad has to **drop** things off to peple and this is why we always have to trek to Lidl!

4. **Drag** means to pull but peple say o what a **drag**! Some pepl say school is a **drag** but i realy like school because it is quite and peacefull there.

5. My **dream** is to get a pet unicorn and to be happy and live in a quite peacefull house. In a candy land!!

'pr' words: press, proud, prove, prefer, pray

1. My mam says you realy **press** my buttons to my dad but my mam does not have buttons! (My mam is not a robot!!)

2. My nanny always says she is **proud** of me and i feel so happy wen she says it and she gives me a Fredo bar and I feel even happyer then!

3. I **prefer** to sleep in my nannys house. It is quite and calm there.

4. Wen my teacher **print**ed my pupil of the week sertificat i was so proud.

5. I **pray** that my uncl will not baby sit me again.

LACES   SANDRA COFFEY

I like girls.' That's how she said it. No preface. No lead-in.
'I like them. Girls.'
Tanya was 12 and I was 11.
She had just shown me for the umpteenth time how to loop one lace over the other 'just like that' and how to do a double knot 'just like that.' I nodded but somehow my fingers couldn't grasp it. I couldn't get the laces to co-operate.

Tanya stayed on her knees in front of me, her hands resting on her thighs. Looking up, she smiled and giggled a little, like someone who had gotten a joke late and didn't want anyone to notice. She was comfortable in that position, telling me the most serious thing I'd ever heard anyone say to anyone.

My friend liked girls. I liked girls too, but this type of liking was different. The way she said it meant so.

'I like to be close to them. How you think about boys, I think that way about girls.'

'I don't think that much about boys.'

'You don't?'

'Not really.'

She grinned. I was convinced an insect or maybe even a family of insects had crept into my ear and fell feet first into my brain, setting off a concoction of panic with their running and racing. *Was this what real panic felt like?* Insects playing a game of catch, their feet beating down on the floor of my thoughts.

How does she know this? I needed to ask her. Without me putting into words, Tanya sensed my question.

'I think you just do. I just do. I know.'

Tanya said it like it was a matter of fact, not open to questioning.

We had sat beside each other in class for the past six years. *Is this something she woke up knowing?* I told myself and my family of insects to calm down. They did a little. This was a time for listening. Real listening.

I hated thinking it, *but would this matter to me in a few months from now?* She was off to an all-girls private school. I was headed for public school. We may not see each other for years.

'I have an idea.'

Now, when I said this, most of my ideas were well ill-conceived. Or 'hard to bring to life'. That was what we said for ideas that were just not quite there.

'We could test it.'

'Test it?' Tanya looked alarmed that I or anyone would want to test her on this.

'Okay, listen. We could get a boy and a girl and go down the back of the old shed like boys and girls do and test this out. Why not?'

'How would that work, exactly?'

'Well, you could be chatting to both at the same time, obviously, and wait to see how your body reacts?'

'Like seriously? Becky, not your best idea.'

'Ultan! That's the boy sorted.'

Ultan was one of those students our teachers couldn't wait to see what he'd be like when he grew up, what he would look like, what he would do. Mothers at the school gates were willing time to go by so they could speak fondly of the time he was in school with their child.

Ultan, that's the boy sorted.

'And the girl?' Tanya asked, right hand on hip.

Okay, as I said I hadn't thought this through fully, but we began to name potentials.

'Anna?'

'She's taller than me.'

'Concepta?'

'She's going to be a nun. She says so all the time.'

'Ah, okay.'

'Geraldine?'

'Now, she's promising.'

'Angela?'

'No way. Those glasses. How does her nose not collapse under the weight of them?'

I was enjoying this.

'Last one. Philippa?'

'Yes. She is so exotic. Her dad is German or French.'

'But, she's cautious.'

'Yes, cautious. And exact. See how she rules her page?'

'Good point.'

'You would need to have everything planned out. She wouldn't follow someone at the drop of a hat.'

On that point, Tanya began to walk. Moving our legs could be just the thing to help us come up with ideas. Like if the thoughts we had in our minds would travel around our bodies and come back to us utterly changed and better. Better ideas. That's what we needed.

I looked at my shoes and how she had tightened the laces tight but not too tight, just tight enough. All four laces facing upwards like bouncy curls with dyed highlights of purple and green for me, pink and yellow for her.

Our school was once a stable yard. On the side of the school shed, a plaque gave some details: Patrick Dempsey. Horse Trainer of Maple Sun. Aintree Grand National Winner 1977. The shed now one long big shelter was used by girls at one end and boys on the other.

The school used it in all their promotional material. Raheeny National School, once home to an Aintree Grand National winner, is today celebrating a Green Fingers Award, A Discover Science plaque and so on. It was a slip of the tongue from a parent that revealed the real reason for its closure. Patrick Dempsey, found dead, suspected poisoning.

The end wall of the playground backed onto a farm and we watched in fits of giggles the grown men herding sheep in and out of the field. Confused sheep were being chased by grown men who punched the air with anger at the animals' lack of understanding of the English language. Minutes later, one of them would pet their sheepdog in such a loving and playful way it was like holding a double picture card, flip it one way for one image, tilt it slightly for another.

Teacher Ms. Furey asked us to look at the field and draw what we saw. *What did we think Farmer PJ was like?* We all had our own ideas. I pictured him sitting by an open fire, eating his soup and brown bread for his evening tea.

'Farmer PJ is looking forward to retirement and spending lots of time in front of the fire.' I wrote this underneath my picture.

'Looks good, Becky.'

Ultan's farmer had a long beard and was standing with two other farmers discussing the state of farming in Ireland.

Tanya's farmer was a woman. Patricia Jane for PJ.

Ms Furey asked her to explain.

'This is Patricia Jane with Emily who is standing in the kitchen and smiling at her. They are about to ...'

'Oh, how very interesting, Tanya. But I don't think farmers would wear high heels out on the farm.'

The boys couldn't put a lid on their giggles, the tops of their bodies, the bits that could be seen above the desk, bobbed up and down.

'We are lucky,' teacher said, that we have a farmer 'so close by'. 'The best way to learn about the seasons is to watch a farmer at work.'

We learnt a lot more than just seasons but Ms Furey never needed to know. I couldn't sleep the night after I first saw a man without a top on. Farmer PJ hired in men from countries like Croatia and Slovakia to help with the busy spring season. Lukas waved to us as he took his shirt off. Our capabilities of turning to utter mush were boundless. When he stopped showing up for work, we spoke about him being in places like Dingle or Bantry, working the fields there. But, we had no idea where he was. A man like that must have had a girlfriend to get back to.

On a warm May day, we sat on the wall with our lunch boxes on our laps and admired how grass could grow just about anywhere. It was even growing on the wall we sat on.

'So, will we try to do something about it?' I asked.

'About what?'

'About you liking girls?'

'Just leave it, Becky.'

'Well, you said you like girls, yes?'

'Yes.'

'You like them, in the same way, I like boys or should like boys, but I don't really think I like boys in that way yet.'

'Yes. I guess so.'

'Are you really sure? How can you be really sure?'

'I just know. Jesus. Why do you have to keep asking? It's just knowing something.'

'Okay, okay. Sorry. Well, do you want to do this? My test?'

'Actually, I have another idea?' Tanya said this and moved in closer as if this plan was such a marvelled idea that it needed to get its first public airing in quiet, hushed tones.

'Tell me!'

'How about we try it on each other? We don't need anyone else.'

'Really? I don't think so. I think ...'

'Why not?'

'It would be better with people you don't know as well?'

'You don't want to help me? This was all your idea, Becky. I'm just, let's say, adapting it to our situation here.'

'Okay. Of course, I want to help you. I'm not sure adapting it like this is such a good idea.'

She made the first move. She jumped down into the long grass. Her smile meant I should follow and I did. My feet barely landed on the grass when she knocked me over and I fell on my side.

'We are not supposed to be out here.'

'Shusssh.'

She moved closer and I didn't push her away. I didn't want to in those first few moments. We were lying side to side, face to face. I could smell her cheese and Tayto breath. She leaned in to kiss me. Her eyes closed, and her lips came closer. I placed my hand on her chest. She pushed gently forward. In that moment, the whole of her body moved as one. Just then I turned away and her lips sucked onto my jaw where she kissed me for what felt like a long time but I'm sure was only a matter of seconds.

I opened my eyes before her. Her lips parted in a smile that I thought would grow into a laugh but didn't. She held it there and let it rest until the moment was long gone. She opened her eyes.

'I told you. Girls are amazing!'

'Are you okay?' I asked. I've no idea why I was asking her. Surely, I should be asked if I was okay? Tanya was consumed by what she had just done. Elated even, like something new inside her was bursting autumn 2018

through in her smile. She pointed upwards towards the wall and we retook our positions.

We never spoke about it. The last weeks of school were filled with exams, preparation for 'big school' and sex education. On our last day, the principal said we were ready. 'Ready for life.'

We said our goodbyes at 2.55 pm on a Friday. We didn't plan to meet up. In fact, it never crossed our minds to arrange it. I boarded the bus and as it drove away I watched her skipping down the road. We never saw each other again.

Twenty years went by. She became the talk of our local town and plenty of others. The papers were stacked on the shop counter and it was there I was attracted to the headline and then the names under the front-page photo. Two women had married, the first to legally do so in Ireland. Tanya was one. Marita, her now wife, was a physiotherapist, and daughter of Lieutenant Marcus Hollenberg, who served on missions abroad. They were both dressed in white, Tanya in a white suit, Marita in a gown with a beaded bodice. They were looking for a surrogate mother. I thought about why she hadn't come looking for me. I'd had three children by then but perhaps she didn't know that even though we had both come back to live in Raheeny.

The months passed. Then the news came. Twin boys born to Ireland's first gay married couple. Aaron and Marcus Junior Hollenberg weighed 5 lbs and 4 lbs and mother and babies were doing well.

LITTLE BOY BLUE   NEIL BANKS

The train I take slows on the overbridge
across Macken Street, past the old flats.
I haven't been this way for – oh, for years.
Below in the grounds, alone, I see
a brown-haired boy in a black coat, running
towards the stair tower with a seemingly
happy shape to him; a little fist
grips a white string tied to a blue balloon
which – as the arm flails about – ducks
and bounces, bidding to find the clouds.
The boy takes high-kneed galloping strides,
his head tilts this way, that; maybe he thinks
he's racing in an Olympic event
or trying to out-pace sheriff's men
across the prairie on his wild-maned horse.
One way or another I keep us both a step
or two ahead of reality.

The scene is brief – my train takes maybe
ten seconds to pass and I never see
the boy's face but still I'm able
to imagine the joy painted there.
I choose Joy, though it could so easily
be the other; it's just we've had enough
of that. As the train passes the flats
on the overbridge and the boy runs
madly across the yard towards the stairs
and a blue balloon bobs against
an uncertain grey background, for those ten
seconds at least one life is perfect.

PIGEON OF PATIENCE   CHRISTINE VALTERS PAINTNER

Each morning
you perch
outside my window,
look out over
the lake of rooftops
wait, puff, coo,
for me to feed you.

Some days I forget,
or rush on, I don't even
like the grey feathers
coated with city grime,
tiny orange eyes, head bobs,
instead I wish for
starlings and sparrows,

but still you return
sometimes with friends,
reminding me of what it is
to hunger and hope
and still I scatter seeds.

BUS-DRIVERS AREN'T BUSES   JAMIE STEDMOND

Cold Coca-Cola from a pint glass.
The day hot, smelling of rubber.
We have a green chopping board for veg,
the one for meat is red.
Plates are askew and untectonic in the sink.
The garden is green growth, untended.
I'm drinking Coke and chopping thyme.
I slice, rocking the knife.

Past double-glazing, gazing, the hedges
are neat and waxy laurel.
Cars are compact.
The estate bisected by a grey length
lined with birch, perfect springy rectangles of lawn.
Primary schoolers in primary colours
pitch and wail; mark
the air with the flutter of runners.

I am 5' 11". Blond. Slight, with a burgeoning gut.
Lightly tanned. My posture is poor.
My mouth is alive with soft sweetness and bubbles
and my arm moves like a crank.
And also not. None of this ...
I am unsprung and deft,
a candent, stowed flicker,
flighty – no less impossible than a bird.

Mutable
and abstract,
clipping repeatedly in elliptical spins
through the prismatic curtain of a waterfall –
I have nothing to do with this.
I am the pilot,
trapped in a craft
off-course.

MRI   MAIRÉAD DONNELLAN

Here they are, brought to light,
details he has not got to grips with,

those articulations she keeps hidden,
the makings of a curve he needs to kiss

as she stoops to fill a saucer of milk,
or draw a splinter of steel from his finger.

Her spine is a column of crockery,
though not the china white he imagined,

he thinks of its slow construction,
curled tight, an ammonite in brine,

the scaffold of her temple, incorruptible,
inching into adolescence and now

he sees the bones he loves are dulled,
the cushions that buffer them have thinned.

In this frame of anatomy and shadow,
she begins to slip into a place he cannot fathom,

still, she is here, carrying man-made words
of hope that come to settle in her head,

like migratory birds, perched on a great cathedral,
as though they know it will hold the weight of them.

CARE TAKER   PAUL BREGAZZI

for George Lawler's retirement

First in, last out,
He swings great steel gates,
Drags and hauls huge wheelie-bins,
Wrestles chair stacks through the door.

He is the wonder of the boys,
On the roof or on the mower,
Or behind the double doors,
Where the boiler purrs and bubbles.

Then he shepherds small ones in a line,
Places in their hands
Papery bulbs or timely seeds

So they follow in his footsteps,
Begging brushes in the autumn
For the sweeping of the fall.
He talks harvest words to them,
Wraps himself round trees for them,
Throws them ash keys to the future.

The air vent in the old school gable whistles out his starling words.
Leaves fall at his leaving.

TASTER   CAROL MCGILL

O nce upon a time there was a princess. I'm not going to tell you what she looked like, or how beautiful she was, because that's not important.

This scene of her story is set in the gloom of a bar, on a night when business was quiet but the regulars were not. A drink had spilled in the corner, the tables were sticky and the paint had peeled completely from the walls. It was dark outside, only a dull glow from the lamps in the street. Nobody took any notice when the princess pushed open the door. A man laughed, but not at her. The princess hesitated, floundered, then made her way to the counter on the back wall. The bartender wore a greying shirt. He raised an eyebrow.

'Can you tell me where Ben is? Please?' She spoke the name like a foreign word. Her hands twisted in the folds of her scarf.

The bartender raised the eyebrow again, this time with an entirely different expression. He nodded at a distant corner. 'Over there.'

Ben was sitting in a booth that was tucked away out of the bartender's eyeline. There was a glass of whiskey on the table in front of him. I am unsure whether to describe this glass as half empty or half full.

The princess sat gingerly on the grubby cushion of the booth, opposite him. She was too young, but Ben couldn't guess her age. The older he got, the harder it was to tell. For several seconds they watched each other.

Finally the princess spoke. Her mouth barely moved, as though she was scared of speech.

'I've heard you can solve problems.'

Ben considered this. 'That's one way of putting it.'

'I've got a problem.'

'Hit me.'

'I'm a princess.'

A pause. 'So ... what's the problem?'

'I don't want to be a princess.'

Ben laughed loudly. Nobody glanced their way. 'Well, that's

something, isn't it? Just like all those old stories. Either they're not a princess and they want to be one, so they marry a prince, or they are a princess and don't like it so they run off with a peasant. What's your problem, girlie? You in love with a peasant?'

The princess dropped her gaze to the glass on the table. 'I don't know how to explain it,' she mumbled.

'Well, you could try.'

Her hands clenched in her lap. 'I have to act a certain way, as a princess. I have to be lovely, and smile, and laugh – I smile so much when I'm with other people,' she said helplessly. 'Smiling doesn't mean anything anymore. I have to be close to perfect. There's no room for mistakes, or for hurting. Because if you're a princess, people judge you all the time.' The words came faster. 'But I always feel like I'm so close to – I'm just *inches* away from – it's like if someone just asked me the wrong question, they'd pull open the cracks in my armour. And I'm not sure who I am on the inside. I'm not sure there's anything left underneath. I *want* to be lovely and kind and generous, but how do I know if I really am those things or if I'm just pretending to be? I don't feel like a person, or I don't like the person I think I am. Even – even when I try to sleep I have nightmares, where misery has a colour I can't name, and I'm straight-jacketed in a tight dress and I wake up screaming. And I can never escape.'

For a moment there was silence. Honesty is often disconcerting. She hadn't wanted to open up, Ben could tell – she'd only done it because she'd thought he would need convincing. The princess looked at the door, then back at the table, refusing to meet his eye.

'You made it this far,' Ben challenged, after a pause. 'Why don't you just ... cut the ropes? Run away?'

'I can't stay here long, they'll notice soon. And I can't run away. I've tried. They find me. They always do. They find me within three days.'

Ben took a thoughtful sip of his drink.

'So what do you want me to do about it?' he asked.

The princess looked up.

'People say you have magic,' she answered, her voice hoarse. Her eyes flicked to the door and back again. 'They say you can make problems disappear. I want you to stop me being a princess.'

Ben sighed.

'Please,' whispered the princess. 'I've tried everything else. Please.'

Ben leaned back so that he could peer over the wall of the booth at the bartender. Then he reached into his coat, and pulled out a tiny brown packet. He placed it on the table between them.

The princess stared at it.

'What's that? Is that magic?'

'Oh yes,' Ben said. 'There's magic in there alright.'

'Will it stop me being a princess?'

She was so eager. These kids, Ben thought, they break your heart.

'Not exactly,' he said. He tapped it with his finger. 'But it might bring you as close as you'll ever be.'

When Ben touched the brown paper the princess twitched, her hand jerking forwards as though to snatch it. No more anxious glances at the door. She couldn't pull her eyes away.

'There'll be a price, you know,' Ben told her sadly. 'And I'm not talking about money. There's always a price for magic. That's like all the old stories too, isn't it? There's a price, but nobody cares about that, until it's too late. The magic always seems worth it.' He paused as the bartender collected two empty pint glasses from a nearby table, throwing grim-faced looks in Ben's direction. 'Until it's time to pay. And the actual magic never works either, does it? It's never what they think it will be. They're double-crossed, or it turns sour, and they realise they were better off to start with. And then they have to pay the price all the same.'

She wasn't listening anymore. He'd lost her attention as soon as he'd put the thing on the table. He could say whatever he liked. But Ben knew just the sound of his voice was keeping the princess where he needed her, reminding her how much she wanted that small brown packet.

'That's how the stories go,' he said softly. 'Magic never works. And princesses are always trapped. One way or another.'

'What do you want for it?' The princess's hand edged forwards.

Ben slid the packet across the table until it rested in front of her.

'That's all right. You can have it. This is just a little taster. See if

41

you like magic. If you do, you can come back any time ... and I'll sell you some more.'

He didn't need to give it away. Giving away was for convincing the wary. She was already hooked. He knew she'd come back. But all the same he let her fold it out of sight behind her fingers, his little act of kindness, while hoping against hope that she wouldn't.

'Just a minute,' he said.

She froze. Fearful, he supposed, that he would take it back.

'All that, just because you're a princess? How do you know that'll stop? How do you know that's not just life?'

The princess tucked the packet away. Ben could see her hands trembling.

'It has to stop,' she whispered. 'It has to.'

She rose and walked unsteadily to the door, across the dingy room, past the tight-lipped bartender. Ben watched her go. Sometimes, when a story takes a certain twist, that's all that can be done.

'Always a price,' he muttered. 'I'm still paying it.'

BLOOD ON THE SHEETS   BARBARA DE FRANCESCHI

What is stillness?
If not a pre-storm delusion.
The first fat rain falls with blithe plops.
Just as hate follows love
a barrage of hail smashes against windowpanes.
Gutters bleed as red earth mixes
with wild gushes of intensity.
Birds nest in oblivion,
safe in foliage designed for natural sanctuary.
Down-pipes ping.
Roof tiles sing.
Sleeping hands awake on a thunder roll
to shield aching bones
from another drunken onslaught.
Sorry is muttered in the early morning light,
a useless word that struggles to breathe.

BEACON   LOUISE G COLE

Where now is that palm-fit sea stone
we agreed was shaped as a lighthouse,
claimed from a wet Welsh holiday beach?
I ran child's fingers along its white helix,
stairs to the flashing beacon, while you

explained the principle of harbour lights
and I wondered if the keeper was lonely
alone on top of cliffs or far out at sea,
didn't know then, until it didn't matter,
white lines in grey were glinting calcite

strata in a bed of limestone exposed
by the ocean's salt water pounding,
time's rough edges all sanded smooth.
Now, another sea pebble on my desk
weighs down a great tower of poems

lamenting your loss, stops the sighs
of a broken heart from blowing them
not seawards, perhaps, but elsewhere.
It's a piece of rock, but not the same
now you're gone, it's just not the same.

BUDDLEIA ON THE TRACKS   RACHEL BURNS

The sun's intensity burns my eyes
I look down and see Buddleia growing
between the tracks, a flush of reddish purple flowers.
The train pulls into Durham station, seven-and-a-half minutes late
confident Dad carries his yellow bike effortlessly onto the train
with toddler daughter, cute as a button, tucked under his other arm.
I stand between carriages next to a woman
with dyed black hair, her arms covered in self-harm scars
and purple to fading green to yellow bruises.
The train travels across countryside, passing
farm land, square fields of wheat and rectangle pastures
with grazing dib dabs of cows and sheep,
then more urban, the terraced houses and smoking factories
high-rise blocks of flats, balconies rammed with clothes
flapping on washing lines, and children's brightly coloured toys.
The train continues its journey towards Newcastle crossing the King
Edward VII Bridge
with the view over the River Tyne, the mirrored glass of the Sage
Music Hall
sparkles in the sun like a disco ball, as if it is singing, *Welcome to All.*

FLIGHT ATTENDANTS   KESHIA STARRETT

we are onboard for your comfort,
  but primarily your safety

birds caught on camera
  still believe they are free –

   not V's trapped under the flightlessness
   of paper-weights;

    I ask swans how they feel about this –
    being folded and alphabetised without consultation

      a magpie tells me she cannot travel anywhere

                alone –

        they will say she *wanted* sorrow

                        please fold along

                          I made you

you tell me sorrow *is* desire
over a cup of tea weaker than

your worn-out knees
and book-like-spine

I hooked my raised pinky finger
around your T9 and tried to turn a page;

left a trail of broken back and lines in margins
I never meant   to make a wishbone out of you

but I mapped your body out

with lines pulled tight –

no slack, for the world to see

the dotted lines

origami

MARCH HARE   KEVIN GRIFFIN

A soft strike on the bumper,
I watch him convulse
and kick three times
as if he is engendering a new life
before he passes.
He relaxes, ebbs away into death,
wide eyes wide, glaze over,
become jewels, for now.

Is that a smile, is it for me.
Are those glassy eyes saying *all right*.
Are they telling me I am the agent,
the instrument of a new creation.
Maybe I am easing my guilt.

I move the body to a green patch
where his world will come,
eat his flesh and scatter his bones.
You will run, March hare,
you will run, again.

WHITE CHALK   MAEVE CASEY

'**W**hat brought you here?'
    You may well ask. What possessed me to come to this
    desert outpost in East Africa, so far from home? A
thunderbolt from heaven that demanded I return to the Christian
fold and go convert the heathen? Not so. Some Pauline conversion on
my road to Damascus? 'Fraid not. Matthew's *I was hungry and you
gave me to eat*. Gimme a break. All that remains with me now of the
Christian is my name, Mary. In fact, it all began in a pub, but then,
being Irish, I accept that life's most noted events often happen there.
As that voice, one new to our noisy crowd, floated my way.

'OK. OK,' he agreed, 'that, I concede'.

'Why?'

'Cause it's true. But then, I'll put it to you, what are *you* doing?' He
seemed to look towards me as he emphasised the *you*. 'Not the
government. Not the EU. Not rich Americans, not the WFP. *You.*'

I knew straight away that he wouldn't fit in with our competitive
and ambitious medical bunch. Whatever made him join us and think
he might have? Anyway, as expected, he left us shortly after, and I
haven't seen or heard of him since. But to my frustration and
surprise, his *you* stayed with me, and despite my futile efforts to
shake it off, stubbornly refused to budge until, until ... well, here I am.

The compound where I now live is situated close by Geneina, west of
the Sudanese Muslim-Christian shaky truce line, close too by the
Chad border. Beyond its low wall, apart from a rusty bay for the
area's food delivery trucks, the desert stretches into middle distance,
its sandy expanse broken here and there by flat-topped acacia trees,
around which small herds of skinny-ribbed goats nibble what little
growth remains. Beyond them, the land dips steeply to a *wadi*, now
totally dry, but given to flood to torrent in the rainy seasons when it
can be crossed, with difficulty, by Land Rover at an underwater stone
edifice known locally as an Irish bridge. Built by ... who? Who, before
me, came this way? None that any local seemed to recall for the
nearby town is peopled by ebony Africans and a sprinkling of

goldskinned Arabs; I, with my reddish hair, pale freckled face and small stature (I stand but five two in my bare feet), remain the outsider, the stranger.

Omar drives me daily as I bring my mobile clinic to the isolated villages scattered beyond the compound's horizon. He converses in good English, and, as the local talk here is endlessly of wars present and wars past he shakes his head to 'there is no god but Allah' and explains that he is a Muslim but 'only a little' and touches the top half of his thumb to reassure me that this is so.

'There is no god but Christus too,' I nod to their shared monotheism. 'And so extremists on both sides kill the other, the believer in a false god. Kill. Kill.' I concede that my name is Christian and he nods in acceptance that I'm 'only a little' that way too.

That sorted, it is now possible for us to do peaceful business together, and so I have a driver and he a job. And I also have, glad to say, now lost my naïve enthusiasm to impose child vaccines, mosquito nets, and all the miracles of twenty-first-century western medicine on a people who prefer to trust their own. So, as of now, I first consult with their elders, include their birth attendants, and make haste slowly.

At my Tuesday village, and while it is still cool, the womenfolk join me in the shade of an acacia tree where we discuss matters food. I chalk their feedback on my large blackboard, how they fared last week with 'cereals', and then onto this week's 'vegetables', their nutritious value, their best mode of cooking, with a touch of vitamins and a dash of minerals thrown in. After, I begin my visits, first call at the hut of a heavily pregnant woman whose baby presents as breech.

'Determined, isn't he? And we've turned him twice already.'

'He says he comes his way. Not head first.'

'It's easier for you and safer for him if he comes my way.'

'You think he's stupid?'

'No, not at all. And the good news is that his development is healthy and his heartbeat fine.'

Five huts down lives a wizened old crone, racked by malaria. I worry, as her wrinkled face contorts with every spasm of coughing, that her once fierce will to survive and care for two AIDS orphaned grandchildren has waned towards a fatalistic acceptance of pending death. Worse still, her older grandson has been badly burnt during his childish efforts at cooking, and cries out when I touch his skin to find a layer peel away and hang, as a large map between my fingers. 'You didn't get him help?'

'And have them take him from me?'

'No, no, I'd run back here to you.'

'You must be brave while I dress this. It'll hurt a little.'

'Noooo.'

'Give him these too, three a day, and even if he improves, you *must* finish them out.'

And so it went, village by village, six days a week, until one morning Omar arrived, later than usual.

'What kept you? I ....'

'Seven villages burnt out last night, and what's more, the food lorries can't get through.'

'So hostilities have resumed? How are my patients?'

'The pregnant one has fled, your older one has died, and her two grandsons have run off to join their militia.'

'But they're just children! And the other villagers?'

'They flee. Some to cross the border, others to follow their animals in search of new pastures, while many set out to walk this way, towards the town. Where there is food, but everyone hoards. To feed their own families first. Then their neighbours.'

'We can hardly damn them for that.'

'Some hoard for profit, for the greater the shortage the higher the price. You understand this greed?'

'Why do you ask?'

'Why?' He shrugged. 'Maybe because you're white.'

He left to scour the town with the wad of money I'd given him and returned footsore early the following day, as I, fingersore, sent evermore emails. And, as the first of the refugees darkened our horizon we argued fiercely as to how we might best share the two sacks of grain he'd managed to buy.

'Women and children first?'

'No. We can't feed them all, it's wasteful to try. We don't give food to those who are close to death, for food will not save them now. Or to those far from death, for they can live on without it for another day. I'll cook a quarter of what we have here, while you, for you are the doctor, will put your chalk to good use, and mark those to be fed today. In that way, we can stretch our food supply to four, maybe even five days.'

'And by then the food lorries will have arrived?'

He shrugged. 'Maybe yes. Maybe no. Who knows?'

I set forth shortly after, white chalk firmly to hand. The refugee numbers had increased overnight and their queue now stretched back to where the land dipped steeply into the *wadi*, while those to the fore faced the lorry bay, eyes pleading, as if awaiting some sacred apparition. I made my nervous way towards them, through the hot sand and to the front of the queue, clammy fingers clutched around the chalk. 'For you,' I said in a determined voice and placed my first white 'X' on a black upturned forehead. Beads of perspiration dripped down into my eyes, as two toddlers were pushed towards me. I quickly shook my head, for they looked healthy enough, and others could share their helping with them if they wished. 'Here, here,' a loud voice called. One toddler still clung tenaciously to my shin, and I felt her small nails dig deep into my flesh. 'Leave,' I commanded, lifted her up, and handed her back to her mother. 'X. Yes to you,' I agreed ... two rows on, 'no, not you, nor you either.' The sun rose higher, sweat pooled at my armpit then dripped down my arm to where the clammy chalk rested. It dazzled my eyes and scorched the sand that rose to fill the spaces between my toes. 'Not you today,' I passed several rows of people, 'none for you either.'

'Give me food,' a youth stepped out into my pathway, 'so I can avenge those who do this to my people.' He grabbed my chalk, eyes enraged, hurled it to the ground and trampled it. White dust rose and merged with sand while those nearby covered their eyes and pulled away. I stood back too to allow a second youth clutch him at the waist and drag him away. Then I took a second chalk from my pocket and moved on. 'You,' I marked a girl I recognised as from the farthest village, 'and you too, and you as well.'

'Not you,' to an emaciated and pot-bellied infant too close to death, 'or you either,' to her frail mother. I began to feel dizzy. The crowd fused to a great mass of unknown peoples, and then, to my surprise, a great feeling of euphoria swept through me. I was as god, for I, yes I, could now decide who lived and who died. I quickly marked another three, a father and his two sons, shook my head to a near-death crone, her healthy daughter and shy granddaughter. Infants were stretched forward, toddlers clung to my legs, a chorus of voices pleaded, as I brushed past them all, unheeding. 'Me, me.' cried a people, desperate for food. 'Yes, you.' He appeared old, but was still strong, the whites of his eyes yellowed and bloodshot. He raised his arm and brushed my mark away. 'Tomorrow, I'll wait 'til then. Thank you. Enough for now.'

I nodded, pleased at what I'd achieved. Had I wasted any grain? No. I'd even been sparing with the chalk.

That night, as I slept, shadows fitfully peopled my dreams. *He was burly, and advanced in years yet his voice was strong as his Kerry vowels echoed round an empire's chamber.*

'Close the ports,' he repeated wearily, 'and retain whatever food we have inside the country.'

'Order. Order.'

'No. No.' The cries echoed back from the crowded benches. 'One cannot interfere with the principles of free trade.'

'Order. Order.'

I woke, to darkness, and struggled to the window. Several mosquitoes that had pitted themselves at the wire mesh lay dead on the sill. The lorry bays? My torch scanned the space outside in futile hope but the bays stared emptily back. Lay down again. Eyes closed. Slept once more. *It was a woman's shadow this time. She queued at US immigration, as three children clung to her.*

'Two children through. No ma'am, he goes back, we don't take none with TB.'

'Alone?'

53

'Lady, he goes back.' His eyes flickered impatiently 'Two in, no more. Sure lady, alone. Let him go, won't live anyways. And what the goddamn use is he to you then?'

'I'm nine now Mama, I'll be alright.'

Her eyes followed him until the white 'X' on his gansaí grew smaller and smaller then disappeared from sight.

Morning brought its bitter dawn as I made my way to the rickety shower, stretched my arm upwards and turned the rusty tap, fingers still white with chalk.

HOT SNOW I AM   MARINA KAZAKOVA

Hot snow I am,
A melting butterfly,
A seagull,
Black and numb,
A burning house
from Tarkovsky's *The Sacrifice*,
A goldfish –
Sogni d'oro! –
Watching the stars
in the aquarium
without water.
You in my dreams
are multiplied –
    a thousand of poppies
besiege me,
stupefied.
You heat my snow,
You melt my moon,
You butterfly me,
You engulf
into the endless
kaleidoscope
    of anticipation.

FLUSHED   ROSA JONES

you roll a strawberry between two fingers.
It is soft and discolouring in

your clutches it reminds me of
the early unsplit fuchsia buds
brimming with nectar at the point
where stem meets branch and

I remember how
I pulled
the heads off all my mother's flowers,
no mercy.

Whimsical children
are often given over to frightening behaviours like that,
now the thought
of pinched ruined buds makes me smile privately, the scratch
of shame finding my lips, a bold daughter lost in a small garden.

You told me that strawberries taste best when they are nearly gone
off, sweetness fermenting,
flavour learning to sprawl out with age left
slightly too long in the sun, sweating.

        I think
I know the secret now,
and now every strawberry I eat will be perfect, overripe, nearly
alcoholic.

The thing
closest to being spoiled is the most delicious but I am
always squeamish
about such things

I need
to keep the mould and dark flies at bay you let them
between your teeth and your tongue
flays the filth away and your smile is all the whiter for it my

stomach cramps nightly and I think you have poisoned me with
fruit that fizzes out in the open, berries bubbling into squalor,
neglected
strawberries that taste like risks.

In photos our mouths will be almost open, jam coloured surely as
you jammed fingers between my lips til I couldn't bear it and they
tasted sour, your kisses
forgotten in the heat, repeated when remembered

I ask you
to leave the strawberries in the fridge so they keep for longer
you ask me where all my verve
and lust for life went I

tell you to shut up, and think to myself that sometimes
rotten fruit is rotten fruit is
rotten is rotten is rotten and maybe

I should take all the new buds in the garden between my fingernails
and pinch
til they split away and leave you
in your punnet to become puree and see
how that suits you, babe.

MOTHER AND CHILD   KNUTE SKINNER

The burping done, he let his body sag
and settle onto her, a heavy weight.

She eased him from her shoulder to her breast,
holding him close but hearing all the while
accounts of murder in the capital
and acts of violence in a far-off land.

Eyes closed and bowels relaxed, he drifted off,
talking in scribbles to her heavy heart.

COW PARSLEY   CIARÁN Ó GRÍOFA

The June ditches are green-drunk
with ancient fern, soup nettle.
In the sudden rain the iron rises.
Cars stir the white cow parsley.

The hill dwellers and their hill hearths
are gone. Still, an old voice echoes:
when the potatoes rotted, it says
the people ate the pignut.

That woody tart root a sop
to salve imagination. Don't ask
what became of the hill dwellers
or where their white bones lie.

One after another the cars
go by; a neighbour lifts a finger.
The cow parsley dances in the thin air.
Deep-rooted. On station. Sinister.

SSH

SINÉAD CREEDON

I've always let silence speak louder than me.

I clock out of the shop at midnight after two gruelling hours of listening to *The Late Debate* on RTÉ 1. Domestic violence was the topic of tonight. My eyes rotated between the door and my lap, avoiding the security cameras where I knew he could see me. If he was in there. I was never sure.

My eldest daughter is up, as usual, when I get home. 'I've put them to bed,' she says without looking from the TV. *The Handmaid's Tale.*

'Thanks, hun,' I say, throwing my keys on the table. I rob the remaining, cold slice of Goodfella's from the plate beside her.

'Mum, what's up?' she asks when I don't hear her or the show. She had been asking me how work was. She had to ask me three times. 'You've been acting strange lately.'

I wrap my arms around her and pull her into me. 'Absolutely nothing.'

I was stocking beans by the office door. I could hear him coughing. I thought about the germs. I dropped a tin. 'Shit.' My hands shook as I cleaned up, scared I wouldn't make it. The door stayed closed.

Brenda came out of the office. She was crying. I had worked with her for the last seven years. She never came back. Brenda was middle-aged and fat.

Eoin was fired before Brenda. He was only eighteen years old and lived only over the bridge. He was working here since he was sixteen. Brenda and I bought him a naggin of vodka when he turned eighteen.

I hadn't left the house that weekend. I showered three times each day. I felt dirty. 'Mum, what's up?'
'I'm not feeling well, hun.'

She wasn't awake when I got home. It was the one night I really needed her to be awake. I was crying. I had mascara on my cheeks. I have not worn mascara since.

'Can I see you in the office?' Derek asked. I smiled at him and followed him into his office. 'It's not great news,' he said, leaning back against his desk while motioning at me to sit down. 'We are going to have to start making cutbacks. Let people go. Less hours. Almost everyone. No one can be favoured, unfortunately.'

I looked at my lap. I didn't like showing emotion in front of people, especially my boss. I held my hands. 'Derek, I have three kids. I've been here for eight years.'

'I can't just take time into account. Even Brenda. I'll have to let her go.'

'You can't do that. She just got her hip done.'

'You know, I don't want to see you go.' He put his hands in his pockets. I looked up quickly, trying to flatten my voice to hide the quivers, looking for hope in his eyes.

He went behind his desk and took a bottle of wine from a drawer. 'Glass?' he offered. I shook my head. He looked disappointed. 'Come on. Have a glass. Maybe you can change my mind.'

He hadn't been my manager for long. He only came in two years ago. He was in his fifties. His belly protruded over his pants and his brown hair stuck to his forehead.

'How?' I asked.

'Just by having a glass of wine with me. Get to know each other a little.'

I had a glass of wine. I drank it very fast. I looked at the little TV in the corner, showing the shop inside. It was empty, apart from Eoin, who was stacking the bottom shelves.

Derek talked to me about me. He told me he always thought I was prettier than other women my age. He told me I don't look like I've had three kids. He told me I couldn't expect anything else, wearing jeans that tight.

He put his hand on my lap.

I said nothing.

He unzipped my pants.

I said nothing.

I say nothing.

There are only two women in the shop now. Me and a nineteen-year-old with boobs. She's very quiet.

ANOTHER ZONE   MARI MAXWELL

Shut down. Reboot. Install driver. Click the download button. Install malware. Download complete. Click to start.
'Zibby, I need a boyfriend.'
'Boy. Friend. I'm sorry. I don't understand. Tell me more so I can help.'
'You know ... Tall. Dark. Handsome.'
'Tall? Wikipedia defines height as the measure of vertical distance. Molasses are dark. Rain clouds are dark.'
'Oh, Zibby! Skin colour.'
'Dark. African. Haitian. Jamaican. Hansom. Two-wheeled covered carriage with driver's seat above and behind. A. Hansom. Born 1803. Died 1882. The engineer/architect who designed it. How else can I help you, Nadee-ah?'
'No, Zibby, no. Handsome. HANDSOME.'
'Reader's Digest Universal Dictionary defines handsome as attractive. You are seeking attractive, Nadee-ah?'
'Boyfriend, Zibby, boyfriend. I know, check the personals.'
'Boy friend. A male child, Nadee-ah. Or youth.'
'Zibby! Jeeze. A sweetheart or lover.'
'Nadee-ah, you are underage.'
'Not a lover, Zibby. Yuck! Someone to go to films with. Eddie Rocket's ... FFS.'
'Eddie Rocket was ...'
'OK, Zibby. Let's start again. You're stressing me out. Now! I'm warning you.'
'OK, Nadee-ah, rebooting system. Momentarily restarting.'
'Ah, Zibby. NOT THAT!'
How ... ow ... May ... Month of Apple Blossom ... how ... Apple ... Goldeeen Deeelish ...
Warning!! System cannot reboot. Nadee-ah, HELK.

HORSE LAKE, GALWAY   PIPPA LITTLE

The day I fed from your hand
like the wild creatures I remembered
coming through the lake shoulder-deep
raising their huge heads over us
so we offered them what we had
and they ate, sweeping their lips across our skin
so my whole arm tingled as if from fever –
then stood a while, looking,
and only an hour later the surface of the lake
was its old grey lilt again
as if those wild souls had never come, or gone:
my hand only, when I pressed my nose in it
remembered them: prickle of sunflower sleeves
and their own scent, green shade of a new-mown damp:
but the day I fed from your hand
I nipped your skin with my teeth, an animal's
warning you didn't notice, the kind of lure
like scraps, rags, anything that gets lost
and catches in fences, but only for a while.

THE ALLEGATIONS AGAINST YOU   KEVIN HIGGINS

after Brendan Behan

This committee finds, in your absence,
that you and your then girlfriend did conspire
together by your vigorousness to disable
a perfectly innocent settee.

We have in our hands a statement –
signed by said settee – which it took us
most of a week and several notebooks to construct.

Though we say so ourselves, our final edit
clarifies your guilt and is a definite
improvement on earlier drafts.

This has been a harrowing process
and everyone involved is exhausted,
especially the settee which, its psychiatrist says,
may never recover from what you two did to it.

Additions to your charge sheet include
that you did, on two occasions, take money
that was legitimately yours from under
one of the victim's cushions.

And that, on April the sixth nineteen ninety four,
you had for dinner two deceased
peanut M & Ms that had been happily
minding their own business down the back
of the violated settee, without seeking,
as you are legally required to, the settee's
written permission.

These most serious accusations will hang
about you like a dead fish under the floorboards
that only you can smell.

Until the hippopotamus, Truth,
rises from the river as it must.
By which time, no matter, you'll belong to us.

IT'S ABOUT YOU   PAUL MCCARRICK

No difference of tone, pitch, or delivery will change the fact
that her name, when said, is the releasing of the Kraken.
Hearing her voice is to take a mid-winter's bus journey at night; her
laugh
(clothes on the line of a fine evening in July) can ease you
into the couch or light the beacons to warn others in the distance.
She is, however, steadily ploughing curls into her hair
of fresh graveyard clay; her hands, a wedding and a wake.
Her face is a modest third edition of *The Old Man and the Sea*
hiding her regrets, pennies in a fountain, anxious to be seen.
And no one can see it as clearly as her.
Her eyes the pure, lethal, learned lines of Brehon law.
But if her eyes were to succumb
to the common law invaders,
her face to become second-hand,
her hair to be left idle or if her hands were to unbecome sacraments,
if her voice broke down on that final stretch home,
or if her laugh were to be drowned in rain,
have no doubt,
her sadness could tarmac Connacht seven times over
and leave no image but black in her trail.

HANDS-ON   JILL TALBOT

W hat else is red? Mom asks as we drive off. Adults always
play these stupid games as a distraction. The sun and the
house are red. Fire is red. Fire hydrants are red. Stop signs
are red, I say.

McDonald's is red, Kiersten says.

Hell is red, I say.

Enough, Mom says.

Jellybeans are red, Kiersten says.

What is blue? Mom asks.

Mom and Dad told my brother Kiersten and me that we're going on a
vacation when really we're escaping the fires that have ravaged
through BC, our entire town being evacuated.

Is everyone else going on a vacation? I asked sarcastically.

Honey, you can't worry about everyone; *we* are going on a
vacation, Mom said.

I know that I'm supposed to go along with these games, being
older, but I can't take pretending that fires are a party. Besides, we're
not the family that sings and goes camping. We are *Little Miss
Sunshine* without the sunshine. We are *Little Miss Emergency* – or
Little Mister Emergency, more likely. Kiersten is five years old,
though he seems more like two. I'm sixteen. But if I hear one more
person say *sweet sixteen,* I'll throw up.

Kiersten already has to pee. We stop at the side of the road. Boys
never even try to hide. The first time the popular girls came to our
house Kiersten said, wanna see my wienie?

Where are we going on vacation? To the first place we can afford to
stay that isn't burning. I put my headphones on. At least I'll have
something to write about for AP English.

I read an article – or a post, pretty much the same thing – saying
that what you grab first in a fire says what kind of person you are. I
grabbed only my phone, which probably just means that I'm not old.

I can't wait to be old enough to move away from here. I mean, to
leave on my own. Mom worries, even though I remind her that we're

white. Honey, you're still a girl, she says. Thanks for the empowerment.

There was a march up this highway for missing and murdered indigenous women.

We stop, and finally I can go on my phone while everyone else is busy with Kiersten's emergency. The internet is already full of the poor lost pets from the fire, and the heroes who've gone looking for them.

It's possible this entire thing is one person's fault. One cigarette butt, one unauthorised campfire – that's all it takes.

We used to sing a song, *He's got the whole world in his hand* ...

How many hands does God have?

We start driving again and I have to put my phone away. We don't get far. Kiersten manages to leave his teddy bear at the side of the road and once we realise this, we have to drive back. We had just left everything and now we have to go back for a bear. He leaves that stupid thing everywhere. The bear has a mustard or puke stain on its mouth and shouldn't be anywhere near civilised people. I'm pretty sure he was adopted or at least from the milkman. Kiersten, not the bear. His hair's all red and he doesn't know how to use a comb. We don't have milkmen but we don't have any random men show up. Maybe he's from an alien.

Dad makes some phone calls and tells several operators that he doesn't want their *support,* that he just needs their help. And why can't anyone help for a change?

Mom says, honey ... and he starts yelling at the operators instead.

After he's done with the operators he starts playing Pink Floyd. Mom makes him turn it off. Dad says, if I knew that being a parent meant giving up ... Mom glares, as if to threaten him to finish his sentence. He doesn't.

You aren't cool, I say, saving everyone.

What's cool these days? Justin Bieber?

Gross, I say.

Mom and Dad look at each other with googly eyes.

Even more gross.

I listen to a *Stuff Your Mom Never Told You* podcast; the episode about hair. Mom tries to act all SuperMom like an ABC Family show but in private she reads depressing memoirs on addiction, obesity and bipolar disease. And parenting books. Stacks and stacks of parenting books. What to tell your kids about dinosaurs, how to introduce your daughter to womanhood, the cyberwar on childhood, etc. I even found one that was called *Yes, Your Teen Is Crazy!* which I did not appreciate. I try to hide any that say teenagers shouldn't have smartphones. You can tell when she's trying to use something she's read – it's like MomSpeak. One book uses the term TeenSpeak and has comics showing how to respond, as if we are the aliens. One time I drew a serial killer into the comic. Mom didn't take it well.

I try to film the fires in the distance along with the red sun but Mom says it's sick and I stop. We pass towns that look like they were made with cardboard, farms and empty space. Americans can pick up and walk to a new life. In Europe they can walk to a different country – a different life entirely. We're surrounded by space. It seems strange that there must've been a time when it was all empty space. And then people showed up and made it into something. The fire in the distance looks like some of the gothic paintings in the museum came to life.

It's possible nobody set the fire. Sometimes things just happen. Sometimes things just happen out of the blue. And then there are operators to support you through the aftermath, and freaks who gawk at the wreckage online, and cat memes.

We aren't religious but I was given a children's bible when learning how to read. Adam and Eve always had leaves show up in exactly the same place, as if by magic. Adam probably built the fires and Eve probably put them out. They were Caucasian with haircuts. Adam looked a bit like James from school. Except James wears glasses and stutters when he speaks to me. It's a good thing we're not really religious because Kiersten thinks *Adam and Steve* are superheroes.

MomSpeak – cover all your bases. A children's bible and a diversity colouring book. It's hard to insult someone who tries so hard. Maybe we'll all go to hell.

Kiersten spills jellybeans everywhere. None of them are red, some are blue.

For Kiersten's birthday he invited one girl to his party. Then he pushed her and she told her mom and it turned into this huge thing. He chose a plastic ring from the treasure drawer at the dentist, then he gave it to the girl from the birthday party, which just made it worse. MomSpeak can be a competition, and she didn't win that one. Mom thought it was progressive that her son would choose a ring and was deeply disappointed when she found out it was for a girl. There are levels – MomSpeak is level 1. PsychoMom is level 5.

The receptionist at the dentist still tells me to get a treat when it's my turn, but says in an irritated voice, you know where it is ...

Maybe it's a test and I was supposed to announce that I was too old for that drawer. If so, I've failed, but nobody is too old for Trident gum.

Teachers made me make father's day cards with little paper ties on white cards when I was a little kid. Now they're too progressive for that. Kiersten gave a card with an alligator on it – too random and stupid to be a problem. Mom and Dad both work for the government. Kiersten is cute enough that it doesn't matter that he's dumb. He even wanted to be a Neanderthal for Halloween, though he gets Neanderthal confused with redneck, and sometimes thinks redneck means having red hair. He doesn't understand any prejudice. There's nothing Mom would love more than to have a talk about prejudice, but I've told her that kids really don't care. Besides, she hates Trump supporters. She says that's different and she doesn't hate them. You just think you're better, I say. She gets flustered. In her books, teenagers are like apes and lack the ability to express anything intelligent.

A giant truck is in front of us. It stinks and is going super slow. Dad swears. Mom tells him not to.

Kiersten starts crying. Mom makes me take off my headphones and play Connect-4 with him – a game probably older than she is. She believes *hands-on* games are healthier for kids. I tell her that no one ever swallowed an iPad.

Most of our *hands-on* games have come from the thrift store, often they have missing pieces. Some kid probably swallowed them.

I put the circular discs in at random.

I already won! Kiersten screams.

We continue driving, playing whatever stupid games Mom can find from her parenting manuals. Kiersten cries three more times. The smoke and haze seem to get worse the darker it gets, even though we're driving away from the worst of it. We get a motel in some no-name town. Kiersten and I share a room.

Can we go to Disneyland tomorrow? Kiersten asks Mom and Dad.

Maybe, Dad says, night night.

Night! Kiersten says.

You too kiddo, Dad says, pointing to me.

Night, I say.

Mom and Dad escape to their room. Kiersten puts on his jammies without even getting under the sheets.

You know we aren't going to Disneyland? I ask.

Yup, he says.

You know there's no Santa?

Yup.

You know Pink Floyd isn't cool?

Yup.

You know we aren't on vacation, we just lost everything?

Yup.

I think of writing a *How To Parent Your Parents* book.

Kiersten quickly falls asleep and into nightmares.

I whisper stories about the characters at Disneyland because sometimes that's all you can do.

His nightmares stop and his terrors are replaced with soft snoring.

I keep telling him stories. Nobody knows it, but Kristoff from *Frozen* actually has a sister. She knows the secret to everything red. Together they can do anything. Together they can combat snow and fire. Together they can find magic jellybeans.

MISOPHONIA   CHRISTINE PACYK

I don't know how it feels
when sound flaunts its colours,
but I witness the explosion of red
when a fork scraping a plate etches
my husband's jaw into granite.
I want you to believe there's no
motion in stone, but I've seen
the way the watery red of a throat
clearing again and again
chisels the fine lines of a wince
and how the blue tap tap
tapping of a foot blanches
his skin to quartz. A squirrel's
piercing chirps erode his vision
to mudslide, so to quell the jagged
decibels of coughs and clicks
and whistles, I hold his hand
and flute pink to him, conduct him
until I feel his unhurried heartbeat,
and together we decompose
all colour, the whole world
dissolving around us
into slippery black calm.

HAWK CROW ADAGIO   STEPHANIE ROBERTS

at this time of year
the local children avoid entering
our small wooded area
mosquitos
stated plain
I cross through anyway for the alone
for the brisk advent of solitude
take the bad with the good
take flabby mood for exercise
take an excuse for emerald bath
and stained glass shimmer

at a clearing on the path
the forest breaks *molto vivace*
abrupt caw crescendo
three black notes cloak and open
three ring riot
a crow sustains itself across the staff
to meet a hawk discordant
like symbols close in prayer
they tussle the hawk mute in the fugue
then a return to corners and rest

I've seen songbirds soar as fists
opposing the apex of their food chain
risking throat almost unarmed
but I'd not seen this
predator to predator and somehow
I manage a mosquito bite
inside the tuba of my ear
the itching – terrific.

LEST SHE DASH HER FOOT AGAINST A STONE
RICHARD W HALPERIN

A psalm in the morning,
A psalm in the evening.

Words are foreign bodies.
A psalm when I got up dispersed
The upside-down of the night.

Heaney wrote 'The Underground',
A film of the soul,
And if the handheld camera shakes,
Of course it does.

Something budges.
Something – Yeats was right –
Dances.

A friend now dead
Seemed to me to be an actual angel.
We would meet over pots of tea.
This is what actual angels must be like.
Solid. Kind.
The dearest psalm
Is a fiction of that.

CAGED BIRDS AT MIGRATION TIME   PATRICK MORAN

In the deepening nights,
they would come back to me,

those caged birds I'd read about
in my big bird book: pining

for flight and breeding ...
zugunruhe.

I could feel them behind the bars,
hopping, whirring, flapping:

helplessly rehearsing
take-offs from their perches;

wings forever straining
across make-believing skies.

THE GIRL WHOSE BIRDS FLEW AWAY
NOME EMEKA PATRICK

it is another night   & the girl's tongue is filled with birds
but the story won't begin this way
        it won't begin with a star & how we all gathered at shore
to watch it   or the moon & how it blazed in our ribs
rather it would begin in the mouth of a gun   & end with a body
drowned in its own blood   or it would begin with the axe
& end with darkness stooping in a corpse's eyes
        it would begin on a Christmas eve   in a cathedral
where a boy says *Hail Mary full of grace*   with a tongue filled with
God
& at the far end   his sister's lips melt into a chocolate bar
he would look at his mother   & smile at the stars in her eyes
he would look at his father   & bow again to continue his prayers
        it would continue where the priest kisses the bible
& proceed to the December sun falling on his face   he would speak
fairly good English   & mutter fairly better Latin
this story would take the shape of a sickle
        & bend into a deadly sharp end   when the bomb rose up
& ate the cathedral into ashes   & the boy is not the boy
& his father is not his father   & his mother is not his mother
& the priest is only a piece   & the girl is a thin thread dipped
& pulled out of fire   & the story will lead us to the girl
whose mouth is filled with wings   when she opens her mouth
every memory of that eve comes flying out   as spears lunched into
bare-soft bodies

THE PAINTER FROM THE TOWER BLOCK   EWA FORNAL

The layers of the thin wallpaper as thin as the butterfly wings, easy to tear, so you could take part in your neighbour's private life.

The colourful crayons I got from my aunt that lives in the US until today. Vibrant and fresh, roll down on the floor. American dream.

At 4 o'clock a.m.

In 1986.

In the tower block.

My father's hands, I have played with.

When he was sleeping, sober only for himself; not for me, not for my mom, not for the world around. His hands my only toys. I baptised them. I was fond of the left one more. For the right one, I didn't care much. The left one never hit me, more intellectual type. A queer maybe? The right one taught me how to fight and how to protect what's mine. They both played a different part in my life.

'The painter from the tower block', that's how they used to call me.

On Sunday aching knees; prayers, white shirt, forgiveness you paid for without delay; preferably with direct debit, if it were only available. To be able to walk out of the church as a decent Catholic man. The innocence FOR SALE but who pays?

During the week, the short breaths in the air. My father is sleeping behind the wall. I'm thankful he is, knowing at least he's alive. With only this thought I wanted to fall asleep and to wake up. But the next day I wouldn't allow him to close the door to the bathroom in fear he might become invisible and walk through the walls like a ghost and leave me, leave me alone.

'LEAVE ME ALONE!' It echoed years later to the ear of a woman I woke up beside, she wanted to touch me and I wanted to be touched, but I was afraid to lose that touch, so I refused to touch or be touched. I grabbed her and bit her lip and pulled her hair. That's all I have, that's not much, that's the way I touch, but I was surprised she was happy with that, she didn't mind.

Some other days in another place, I lay on my stomach inhaling the floral scent.

'Would you like me to give you something to cry about today?' she asks.

'Yea very much.'

'I want to give it to you, squeeze tears out of you, but that's between me and you,' she whispers, 'otherwise I'm at risk of losing my licence.'

'That's between me and you,' I repeated after her. 'And I swear, I won't tell anyone unless it tells itself one day, but even though it does, you're still safe.'

Today I'm confused about what I should and shouldn't share. Will somebody tell me what are the proper settings? Whose life is private on this planet?

There was always someone who saw what happened to you and didn't do a damn thing to stop it. Is this private? Someone that contributed to what you are and what you are not. The school was that place. They have shown you what you're not in the first place. They kept saying that until you forgot what you can be and what you are. In the end, they asked if you could keep shut your beautiful mouth. It's 'a private matter'. When the fact is, IT'S NOT. It's a public matter you've been just left with.

ON YOUR OWN.

The red-hot streams down from your nose. You've been thrown against a wall of YOUR OWN INSIDE. Now your health is a public concern.

What I got out of my country, the bunch of flowers grown out of the communist concrete slapped in my face like Sharapova's racquet. But the crayons made my way out of it. I drew the new world, I drew the home without the walls, I wanted to live. Otherwise, I wouldn't be able to speak, I wouldn't be able to breathe, I wouldn't be able to be back to who I can be. And I know that finally I CAN BE ME.

UNHEARD MEMORIES   JESS RAYMON

Saturday I wake in bed. I find my rose-freckled body naked and covered in dirt.

At first, I mistake the gritty bits of grass between my fingers for flowing voluminous hair. Time feels breezy and light, like I'm in the back seat of a red convertible headed for the beach. Only, two hard nipples poke through sleep's fog and cause it to break. I'm left with ringing ears and a throbbing nose.

It seems a tornado spun a few laps through my small brick cottage and fled the scene. When? I don't know. The beige carpets and eggshell walls are covered in foot and handprints. I dress in pyjamas and follow them. I encounter brown balls shooting urchin-like green spikes, in obvious spots, like on the lilac kitchen countertop, and in confusing spots, like along the dust-crusted bookcases in the spare room.

Outside, the scene smells of biblical revenge. I stand, shivering, arms crossed in disbelief. Everything is uprooted: beetroot weaves in to the world of dangling peas; carrots, unearthed and broken, rub up against confused potatoes. It is unripe vegetable speed dating – uncomfortable, exposed; exasperation cloaked in a past.

The fuck went on? My stomach, a sturdy and reliable organ – my favourite organ even – feels pummelled and queasy. I've not felt this outside of myself since that day I found him in the bathtub.

My phone buzzes.

Louise: Time will I collect you for the girls' recital tomorrow? xx
Me: Was there a big storm last night?
Louise: Is 4pm ok? Need to be there early to drop girls off. No storm, x.

Louise was the one who insisted I start tending vegetables a few years back. She thought I needed to nurture and care for something. A 'project'. No one mentioned grief. But to my own surprise and maybe irritation, I enjoyed watching the small green spheres – weightless buds, tiny possibilities – transform into edible rainbows.

79

The sun peeks through the cloud cover and a spotlight beams down onto the garden. I see a twinkle appear in the vegetable patch: there's something shiny buried in the far right corner. I bend down, sinking my striped-cotton pyjama knees into the soft cool earth, and perform an archaeological dig around the metal bone that pokes out from the ground. Carefully, I paw the soil into a mound behind me.

After a few minutes I expose a trumpet: inedible and not yet rusted; in fact, it looks relatively new. I never liked brass, myself. Not then, not now. Mouth spit vibrations feel too intimate and invasive, too sloppy. He had loved the saxophone but I could never uncoil like he could.

My phone vibrates again.

Louise: Ellie, is 4pm alright tom??? Please don't let the girls down.

Suddenly, a fluid erupts from my kidneys and creeps into my thin rose-freckled limbs. I lose all strength. I flop the trumpet onto the soil and myself onto the sofa inside. I wonder if I should have listened to the doctor with red curls and burgundy-rimmed spectacles pushing lithium. It's hard to know who to listen to.

A few hours later I wake to a ring at the doorbell.

Through the peephole I see Keith Cohen. Clad head to toe in vintage rugby gear, he hops from foot to foot as he waits for me to answer. When I open the door I notice that his face, tan and square, wears a scrunched nose and rippled forehead, bringing the two chocolate brown caterpillars above his eyes closer to one another, as though inching towards a kiss.

'Ellie, you well?' Keith asks.

I try to nod. 'Alright Keith, you?'

'Exhausted. Fucking wrecked. What in god's name were you doing out the back last night?'

'Ah, sorry, I ... I don't know. I must've been sleepwalking, I don't remember.'

'Christ, you're having a fucking laugh.'

Caterpillars pull tighter.

'Yeah. Must've been. I can't really remember.'

'Fuck me. Sleepwalking?'

I count the squares on his top and wish he'd go.

'Were you proper wasted again? No one plays trumpet asleep. Fuck's sake. I was close to ringing the guards. I'd have been well within my right to.'

Caterpillars nearly unite in passion.

'What?' I feel sick. 'I don't play the trumpet, Keith.' My neck goes stiff and pain shoots into my right nostril. I taste dirt.

'Well, it sure fucking sounds like you do, bloody loud.'

'Was ... was I?'

I scratch my ears.

'Listen, it was you. Liz saw you from the bedroom window. Maybe you'd had too much red again and blacked out, but don't give me this I-did-what shite.'

The caterpillars' passion wanes. The lovers retreat.

'I know it's not been easy for you, with Michael ... you know, gone. But I have to look after my own family. It took Liz two hours to get Emma back down, like.'

'I know ... but I didn't, I'm sorry. I don't remember.'

'Alright. But Jesus, Ellie, leave the trumpet alone after midnight!' His square body turns and fades away.

***

Sunday I wake on the sofa. I find my body covered in yesterday's striped-cotton pyjamas (now with dirt-patched knees). A begonia glow wrestles out through rows of chimney caps. Trumpet keys. The light pierces in, scans the room and settles on my legs.

I turn on the telly. My remote control selects a BBC African elephant documentary. Attenborough. A herd of twelve is taking a playful bath together in a muddy red pool. Trunks spray thick water over each other's wrinkly masses. My breathing slows. The animals tease each other and flap flies away with their paper plate ears. Yesterday's lurid memories drift away.

It's been a good while since I touched other humans. Not sexually. Not non-sexually. A while back I'd tried (mostly sexually) but it made my body stutter like the motor on an old fishing boat. Observing these wild creatures, I imagine the warm weight of several trunks, covered in prickly black hairs, wrapping around my waist. The tight trunks squeeze and warm elephant breaths light a spark down my lower spine.

Eleven minutes later the credits run. Attenborough moves on to primates.

A ripple of pain takes my upper chest. That herd is still together, carefree and playful; I am alone.

The fuck is going on? I need to get out. Move. *Something.* I walk out of my estate and head for town. The orange bricks crackle and erode against the sharp blue sky. The air is fresh, and the scent of sweet cedar burning in the distance is strong but untraceable.

Once at the shops, I get tea and a raspberry scone, and then sit down. Both items disappear. I assume this is my doing but I'm not sure. I walk along the busy road, notice shops I didn't know existed, but nothing seems real, nothing sticks to anything, like trying to read a novel after a bottle of Cabernet.

I see a sign. Plum text on a bronze plaque, it reads: *Ancestral Answers.* Looking at the daffodil shop front I have the strange feeling of having been here before. It could be the pink geraniums in the planter pots below the window. Louise has those at hers. When she was only small, my eldest niece picked one and handed it to me. Louise gave out to her for it.

My arms, under some sort of trance, open the shop door.

My neck feels clammy. A receptionist with chubby wrists and gold bangles asks me if I have an appointment. Then for fifty quid – could take up to forty-five minutes, she says. I follow her to a small backroom where heady incense spirals under low light.

He arrives wearing a dark robe, hood down, revealing the early stages of a balding head. Baggy cheeks hang from his shiny round face. As he sits down at the table, his motions are slow, almost delayed, like he's concentrating too intently on each tiny movement, like he's trying to slow time.

'Ellie, is it? Lovely to meet you. Please sit,' he says. 'First time here?'

I nod once. He nods three times.

'Is there a specific question you've come here with today? Is there a loved one, maybe, you've been trying to contact?'

'No. Well, not really. I don't know. It's all a bit fucked. I woke up and there's all this dirt, loads of it, everywhere. And I don't remember anything. I wasn't drinking, like. Keith was really fucked off about the noise, the trumpet music. He's my neighbour, always been a prick, even to Michael. But it might have been me. Playing the trumpet, I mean. I don't remember. Then Attenborough came on and these lovely creatures, elephants, were playing together – it was like I was there inside them. I was part of their herd. It's fucked up. I don't know. I just wish I could remember. Is that what you do here? Help people remember? My ears are screaming at me, like an infection and a kick in the head at once. My nose too. I don't –'

'Sh. Now. Let me take a look. Do you mind?' he asks, indicating my head with his right hand. I nod and he closes his eyes. He hovers his hands, palms together, over my face, stopping for almost a full minute over the top of my nose. My breath reflects off of his hand.

'Does it feel like something is missing here?' he asks, pointing to my nose.

'There's pain.'

He excuses himself and leaves to a back closet, telling me to wait. I hear scuffling.

He returns several minutes later with a book, a solid black hardback with thick dust on the cover. Opening the book, he stops on page twenty-two. There sits an adolescent girl, pale skin, curly auburn hair, a flowery summer dress and an elephant's trunk.

I scream.

'Sh, sh, sh. It's alright.' His tone grows softer. 'Next one.'

Page 73: an older Asian man in his eighties, tousled salt and pepper hair, loose trousers held up by suspenders, elephant ears.

'Fuck! Is that what's going to happen to me?'

'No, no. Not to worry. These images are only a metaphor for how your soul is expressing itself. You are experiencing a tiny hiccup in the miracle of reincarnation. Your body managed to evolve to its next life, but, you see, there's unfinished emotional turmoil in your soul from a past life as an elephant.'

My heart tempo is fast.

'This usually happens later in life, often after a traumatic event, like illness or death. The elephant soul from your past life is re-emerging and that's why you feel too much energy in your ears and nose – your soul is trying to grow back the bits the physical body lost.'

'Can you make it go away?' I rasp, not believing in my mind but believing in my ears and nose.

'We offer group counselling, once a week – Tuesdays at the moment. Not everyone is experiencing the same past life trauma, naturally, but it's a very supportive and encouraging environment. We conduct group discussions on the topic of unresolved soul stagnation. It will help you connect with your past self and figure out what needs healing. Hold on – I'll get you a brochure and some details.' He stands up, offering a careful smile in my direction and turns to the closet again.

***

Back on the street, I jog away from humans and group meetings. My heart pushes me towards a crescendo of trumpets. Everything else becomes the scone: raspberry and forgotten.

A dense and prickly trunk will wrap around my waist and pull me deep into the soil.

BOSCH'S OWLS   REBECCA GETHIN

There must be one somewhere
among the blur of trees beside the river bank.
It's rare there isn't one.

You can sense it waiting
for the worker-angels to stop their fanfares
announcing the arrival of another cargo,
accompanied by an egret and what looks like a drongo,
to the island of no-escape, of endless dusk
its mindscape the wrong side of skin.

A little owl would bring peace;
a barn owl, shroud white, the safety of wisdom;
a tawny owl with its hellish shriek
the comfort of uncertainty;
an eagle owl with its two-note call
a reminder of breathing.

He hears it calling – there, among the foliage,
just outside the frame perhaps
or not yet formed and soon to be flying in
to settle on a branch –
    herald, messenger, bird of prayer.

BEYOND RED HILL   PETER BRANSON

Back here, what lies beyond this place, field, stream
and wood, is wilderness, intense, compared
to half-day closed all week, small market town,
mean streets he wastes our early childhood in.
Long holidays are perfect clear blue skies,
enchanted time, off on his bike all day
with mates, the pedals proud against his feet,
on sunken winding tracks and bridleways,
down splashy Watery Lanes, the Downs beyond,
sublime, the prospect of no school for weeks,
till stifling afternoons oppress. Beside
himself, short fuses, bullying, ashamed,
he's pitching in, weird tingling deep inside,
dark chocolate bitter on his tongue, inspired.
Black clouds are gathering above Red Hill
like thunderheads: strange potions simmer in
the blood. The ladders yo-yo, pleasure – pain,
old nightmares stirred by rote, the snakes attract,
where parents, teachers, wield words-to-the-wise
like weapons, razorblades inside his brain.
Cheap perfume on the breeze, illicit pint,
prop cigarette, he's gazing longingly
at city lights some twenty stops away
projecting on the summer evening sky.
Raw promise of excitement, danger, sex,
he dreams of soft white flesh he's glimpsed above
dark stocking top beneath gyrating dress.
If we could charm dark energy to slide
beyond space-time the quantum way, what would
      they make of me, d'you think? What could I say?

AUBADE   CLARE SAWTELL

June 21ˢᵗ 2018

There's a branch in the wood
where the sun never shines
except this day.
It's moving slowly in the morning.
I can just see it
through the trees.

MRI scan this afternoon.
Magpies have such beautiful wings
when they're outstretched.

May what needs to be seen be
seen and what doesn't
remain uncovered.

THE IRISH SUMMER, 2018   RUTH QUINLAN

There was an unexpected scarcity,
an absence of water in this country.
We, the waterlogged folk, a people
of knitted jumpers pearled with drizzle,
muck-spattered wellies in sucking fields,
cloud-banked skies and bursting heavens,
a thousand fond expressions for rain,
fumbled with the language of drought.

The reservoirs were drained out, empty,
silverfish scuttling in shadows
chasing tastes of tidemarks.
The umbilical cord to liquid severed,
we lived like lesser gods, suppressing
yearnings to lick the walls of caves
for a tongue-slick of moisture,
to retreat from the glare and hide
like troglodytes, do anything
to stop the frying
like over-stuffed sausages,
greased and salted with our own sweat.

RED WITH A PURPLE STRIPE   HANNAH VAN DIDDEN

Her grandmother had spoken often enough about it with her so, when the orange-topped mushrooms came into view, Merisse knew this was the place. This was where the fairies played with the frogs, in amongst the mushrooms and lavender and the nuts with star-shaped cutouts inside. At the very back, beyond the field of gnarly garden, was a rickety lean-to propped against a paperbark, surrounded by gravel and thin-twigged brush and leaves to be swept. She inspected the wooden shelter with pride and claimed it with the setting down of her Dora the Explorer backpack. This was where she would live. This was her place now.

She had left the family home and she couldn't go back. She wouldn't go back.

'How could you?' she'd cried at her father, and he had been confused.

'It's just an empty plot. Your grandma had a vision for it, Merry, but she passed on before – '

'It's not empty! Where will the little folk go? Did you even think of them?' She was shouting at him, but he seemed not to hear because he'd grabbed her into him and her screams were lost in his duffle coat.

'She's gone, Merisse. She's gone,' he said, and he stroked her head three times before she realised what was going on.

No, she would not be placated! She wriggled from his grip and escaped to her room. At first, she cried – but she knew this would do no one any good. She had no time. Saving the little folk was a serious business. And she was forming a plan ...

Merisse spread out the tablecloth from her pack, setting it with plates and cutlery and pilfered jars and packets from home: water crackers; a bag of apples; two bananas; the last slices of bread; the last spoonfuls of strawberry jam; a jar of pickles (the tiny ones); a plastic bag (for rubbish – in the bush you shouldn't take more than pictures or leave more than footprints, as she well knew). And she had her father's secret stash of chocolate fudge cookies that she was allowed only on special occasions.

She was old enough to understand about refrigeration and perishables. The food wouldn't last her long, but at least it would last in this weather. They were having a cold spell.

'Do you know what a cold spell is, Merry?' her grandmother – otherwise known as Fred, short for Frederica – would ask. Even though Merisse did know, on account of being told the same story at the weather's every downward turn, she let her grandmother explain.

'A cold spell is when one of the trolls gets a hold of a fairy spell book and tries to do some magic of their own.'

'But trolls can't do fairy magic!' Merisse had interjected at the first telling.

'I know that and you know that,' Fred said. 'But that doesn't stop those trolls from giving it a go! They always get it wrong though, don't they?'

'Can trolls even read?' Merisse had asked during the last cold spell talk.

'Some can.' Fred nodded. 'Most can't, but they can do enough to cause a chill by tracing their fingers over the golden letters of the spells.'

'Is that what happened to you?'

Fred eyed her strangely.

'Dad said you caught a chill and that's why you're here. A chill is a cold spell, isn't it?'

'Yes. I guess it is something like that.'

'When will they let you go back home?'

Fred produced a hand from the crisp cotton bedclothes and touched it to her granddaughter. 'Quick! You'd best go before the matron comes to take you away. She'll give you less mercy than a tree goblin.'

Tree goblins. She had forgotten about them. They came out when it was dark, and they would rattle and bump and whoosh through the branches so you would think it was the wind, but really they were biding their time before –

Whoo, whoo.

Phew! An owl overhead. The only thing that could possibly frighten a tree goblin.

'Thank you, Mrs Owl,' Merisse said, but not too loudly: she didn't want to scare off her protector.

The dark was closing in now but she was prepared. The tablecloth doubled as a groundsheet, and she had her dad's very good, rated-to-Antarctic-conditions sleeping bag. And she had taken the woollen beanie he had made when he was supposed to be teaching her how to knit on a weekend craft day.

'It's too hard, Daddy!' she had said, loosening the half-hearted loops from her needle.

'You've only just started, my little one.'

'But I'm tired.'

'Okay,' he sighed. 'Go to bed and I will get you started again tomorrow.'

She woke the next morning with the finished product on her head – red with a purple stripe, just as she had wanted.

'Red for Fred,' he told her.

'And purple because it's Mum's favourite colour,' she said. 'But where is your beanie?'

'I decided to make yours first. Do you like it?'

The beanie was cosy warm and fuzzy on her head and she was glad to have it. At the time he had knitted it, they had been going through another cold spell. But not like this one. As night set in, the air hung in clouds from her face when she breathed. She tucked herself deeper into the sleeping bag, pulled the beanie further over her ears and eyebrows. She felt icicles form on the tip of her nose.

Merisse listed those things she had left behind: her scarf, her best coat, her gloves. Her mother's old gloves. She regretted leaving them. Dad would chuck those out like he did with the rest of mum's stuff and that could not be helped. There was only so much that Dora the Explorer and her bike basket could take, and the sun had been warm on her back when she set out.

'Is fairy magic strong?' she asked, in the time before Fred had been taken from her house by an ambulance. She already knew what an ambulance was. Her class had an incursion in one and she got to try out the oxygen mask, and she knew oxygen was good for you, so she wasn't worried when they attached the mask to Fred.

'Oh yes, Merry,' Fred had replied. 'The strongest of all.'

'Could it make you better?'

'Maybe.' Fred smiled. Then she coughed.

'Maybe if I asked, the fairies could bring back my mum.'

'Oh,' said Fred, 'but that would require every ounce of their might. You would have to find their home, to find the source of their powers. And when you find them, you have to seek out the fairy queen. Her name is Ambrosia.'

Merisse mouthed the strange name. 'But how will I recognise her?'

'You'll know her when you see her.' Fred winked at her. 'And when you see her, give her my love, won't you?'

Then she told Merisse about the fairies' secret land – the bush block and the mushrooms – and, a short time after that, Merisse overheard the conversation that told her the block was being sold.

They couldn't sell it while she lived here, she was fairly sure of that. The man who used to live next door had taught her that.

'Squatter's rights!' he had yelled at the police who knocked down his front door.

Besides, it was destined to become hers. Fred had said so. If she stayed and told them, 'There's been a mistake and it's not for sale,' they would have to let her keep it because she was the custodian. It was her job to keep the little folk safe.

On the afternoon that Fred passed, Merisse rode her bike to the hospital and locked it to the bike rack outside Emergency, as she had done for numberless days. She said, 'Hello, Penny,' to the receptionist in the main reception area and headed down the corridor to the lifts. Then she walked into the ward that held her grandmother. She paused to greet the duty nurses who were too busy talking to acknowledge her. By the time they had realised who she was, by the time they had lunged her way, she could not be stopped: Merisse had planted herself at the entrance to Fred's now-empty room.

'Did you let her go home?' she asked, the face of her handpicked sunflower tapping at her tights.

Merisse wouldn't believe her father when he said Fred had died. They cried into one another's necks and she did not remember getting into bed that night, only that she woke in the comfort of her eiderdown quilt.

She conjured it to mind – her bed with the stuffed heart on the pillow – as though it would make that memory of comfort and warmth real, and she would have grabbed hold of it too, if it wasn't for the twigs snapping overhead. Tree goblins. And this time, not an owl in sight. She set aside her dreams of bed and sleep and widened her eyes, otherwise unmoving, which wasn't hard: her limbs felt like they were frozen solid. She decided Antarctica must not be a very cold place after all.

In spite of the threat posed by the tree goblins, she was barely conscious when she saw the lights.

Wood sprites! They just had to be. Now wood sprites could be temperamental, but surely they would help if they could see the trouble she was in.

A larger figure emerged from between the sprites, moving slowly back and forth, away. Away?

'Ambrosia! Don't leave!' Merisse called, and the figure stopped. 'It's okay. Fred told me about you.'

Her eyelids fell and she smiled in the fairy queen's direction through the tangled growth and mist. In moments, she was clamped and lifted from the ground.

'Fred gives you her love,' she whispered.

When Ambrosia spoke, the voice was familiar, nothing like she had imagined.

'It's her! She's here!' The voice reached over her shoulder and a buzz grew all around, the other lights closing in. In gentler tones, she heard, 'Merry, you're ice cold,' and this voice was her dad's.

'Dad, I have to stay.' She shivered in the crook of his arm. 'I saw her.'

'Never mind that. We need to get you home.'

Through her still-shut eyes, she became aware of shadows dancing around her, of needles in her hands and pins in her feet. And she saw bright lights float above her, flashing different colours. The wood sprites were saying their goodbyes in a rainbow.

Her dad wasn't angry. Merisse thought he would be, but he wasn't. Not at all. He stopped going to work after that and she stopped going to school, and their weekend craft days happened on weekdays. Beside her dad on the block that was no longer for sale, she did her lessons, and she learned how to saw and drill and paint. And she learned to knit.

When the next winter came, she knitted him a beanie. Red with a purple stripe. Cosy warm and fuzzy for those cold spells in their new log cabin.

THE CRANNÓG QUESTIONNAIRE   FIONA SAMPSON

How would you introduce yourself as a writer to those who may not know you?

I seem to have eras, both in my writing and in how my writing is thought of. I find that a bit confusing, because I *feel* like myself all the time. I think I'm always trying to work in the same direction. I mean, of course one has imaginative spells and dry spells and rational spells too. But my ideals, around books, art, poetry and society, have never really changed, although I've developed and changed out of all recognition, and my working life and the opportunities I've had to write have also changed enormously.

I'm a poet, and that's I guess what I've had honours and awards for, here and abroad. I do a great deal of work in other countries, where I'm much translated, and where I also work with other poets to support their work into print. I co-translate, and have worked as a literary editor. I've also done lots of reviewing. I'm the kind of critic who doesn't get high on trashing someone (which is so easy), but who tries to pay attention to what's *really* going on in a book, even if I don't think it's fully successful. I was that kind of editor too: the kind who always reads everything in the slush pile and doesn't practise nepotism. I'm not sure such good practice has much of a place in contemporary British poetry, but it certainly does in the rest of the literary world ...! Before all this, I worked with writing in health and social care for years.

But I've also always been a prose writer manquée and now I've published three prose books in the last two years. A literary biography, *In Search of Mary Shelley* (Profile), came out in January and has had just a wonderful reception, and last summer I published a book about *Limestone Country* (Little Toller), which I'm also very proud of. I love writing about place. And at the end of 2016 *Lyric Cousins: poetry and musical form*, which EUP have published in paperback this month, so it's now out in an affordable way (it was £70+. Pointless).

When did you start writing?

I gave up the violin when I was twenty-three and launched myself into writing. I had no idea how hard it would be in every way. But I'm glad I didn't know: or I wouldn't have had the courage to do it. And it is who I am. I'm no essentialist, but I do know that this way of going on suits me as nothing else does. I'm not a career scholar, though I love doing scholarly research – and then turning it into a great story. I'm not an entertainer: I am entertained, or engaged, only by serious writing. I'm not simply a musician: I love language. But I am a writer.

I wrote stories and poems in my village primary school, where I knew I wanted to be a writer and no-one, in that innocent time and place, told me it wasn't for the likes of me. But my teens in not-specially-good Welsh and English state schools with, latterly, an English teacher who hated me – and the realisation that as a girl much was closed to me – knocked that out of me and I made a foolish detour (into music) for some years. I had some amazing experiences but I bitterly regret the handicap of being a late starter in writing.

Do you have a writing routine?

Not as much of one as I'd like: I rely on fierce organisation and time management to get things written. I've always had to support myself, so the day jobs have always been with me. But I do write first thing (which on uninterrupted days, and in the absence of any intervening crisis, means most of the morning), and on days when I'm writing I go for 1,000 words a day. Poetry isn't quite like that but it too is a first-thing routine. I write it before getting out of bed in the morning.

I'm someone who relies heavily on deadlines and timetables. I love writing – you don't have to drag me to it, though you may have to drag me away from it – but I can't write if I believe no-one is going to read the text. A kind of terrible lack of confidence enters it.

When you write, do you picture somehow a potential audience or do you just write?

Oh, I just started to answer this above! I do picture an audience: for prose, anyway. I feel that I'm talking, persuading, explaining *to you*. If I'm on automatic pilot for any reason, I tend to notice it by picking up that I'm just boring, rather than charming, this ideal reader. I think poetry is much less advertent, much less sociable, in its instigation though. I don't think that I write it *to* someone, but simply *from* myself.

Some writers describe themselves as planners, while others plunge right in to the writing. Would you consider yourself a planner or a plunger?

A plunger! Despite all that I've said so far, I know that the important thing is not displacement activity, but writing. And in writing I always find I say more than I knew that I thought. I'm much more interesting on the page than in life, for example. Though this may be because one gets in the girlie habit of not talking about one's stuff but instead listening ...

But I plunge with a plan or direction. Both in poetry and prose I have a sense of making through doing, but also at the same time of shaping a given direction. In poetry, I concentrate on the poetic thought (that's not an epithet! It's just a category – the matter of the poem) but it's being shaped as it goes by technique. In prose, I plunge in, but it's being shaped as I go by my book- or essay-plan.

How important are names to you in your books? Do you choose the names based on liking the way they sound or for the meaning? Do you have any name choosing resources you recommend?

Not being a fiction writer, no. Although I changed many of the names of the people in *Limestone Country*, in case they didn't like what I'd written about them (though I didn't feel I wrote anything disparaging. But you never know). It's a book about inhabited landscapes: the push and pull between person and place. So being observant, rather than sweetly charming, about the people in them was the whole point. I tried to translate these names sideways, to get a similar feel. For example a French farming family had in real life a surname from a village in the Vézère valley: I picked another hamlet from the same region, whose name had similar metrical attributes, as their pseudonym.

Is there a certain type of scene that's harder for you to write than others? Love? Action? Erotic?

I find it hard to write narrative verse. How do you move things along without ending up writing tranches of exposition? But I have worked with long poem form (I wrote a verse novel in 2006) and am working on a libretto right now; so I don't duck the issue!

Tell us a bit about your non-literary work experience, please.

I have worked in literature ever since I stopped being a violinist. But especially when I was in my twenties I was very committed to community arts practice. So I didn't just work with writing in health and social care: I worked in adult ed (teaching feminist theory as well as the inevitable creative writing) and did what must have been hundreds of schools' workshops. I also set up an international poetry festival that was deeply rooted in the community itself (Aberystwyth, in Wales). All of this had to do with my belief in 'bread and roses': that the good things in life, the things that bring pleasure but also give meaning, must be available to *everyone*. The professional and indeed personal economic costs of this idealism were rather too high (another thing I didn't know when I was young) but there was some artistic pay-off. I have been fearless ever since in advocacy of access to really good provision for everyone. I don't think it's elitist to make the best writing, art, music, drama available to everyone, rather than fob people off with dumbed-down pap. I think the fobbing off is what's elitist and patronising. What I found was that – laid open by the great and awful events in life – everyone, including people who have never had any prior relationship with anything 'arty', wants and needs and understands the best, the greatest, work. *And they deserve it.*

I also became quite politicised in a different direction by work in the Balkans. I became very committed to translation and cultural translation as key to dialogue between equals. My partner for a long time was a writer who had a 'bombing cancer', one of the soft tissue cancers that occur in clusters of cases in the places where NATO bombed former Yugoslavia (and other countries, incidentally) using depleted uranium as ballast. I am deeply moved by the Balkans and can't believe how they are simply regarded as unfashionable by western culture-makers now. Those fault lines haven't gone anywhere. They are all still waiting for the next seismic shake-up.

What do you like to read in your free time?
Much of everything!

What one book do you wish you had written?
Apart from Proust/Joyce/Eliot, do you mean? The list is just too long ... I can't possibly pick one. Oh, *Vixen* by W.S. Merwin is probably my most specific poetry model; *Danube* by Claudio Magris non-fiction; *The Bridge over the Drina* by Ivo Andric the novel ...

Do you see writing short stories as practice for writing novels?
I'm not qualified to say, as I don't write fiction. But I think young writers in the US are lucky that there are still amazing outlets for short literary fiction: as the form, though exquisitely controlled, *is* concentrated. It *does* allow a young writer to reach a real audience before they're either ready or allowed to have a book. Small wonder, too, that their short fiction is so good.

Do you think writers have a social role to play in society or is their role solely artistic?
Yes, I think writers do have a role to play. One such is simply, as I've tried to help in a tiny way towards doing, to make the written culture open, inclusive, accessible, a genuine place to discuss and to hear discussion by a chorus of voices.

But I've also worked enough in countries other than philistine, anti-intellectual, muddling-along-blindly Britain to know that in most other parts of the world writers are public figures with a remit to think and feel for their societies. We might even say their societies think and feel *through* them. I think that's incredibly important. Look at the Anglophone societies who don't have such figures – UK, US, Australia – who, despite their western comforts and liberties seem to confine public discussion of ideas and events to politicians and journalists, and you can see how fatally reductive of the discourse that is. And the consequences for, among other things, democracy. We desperately need thinkers who are not political careerists or their accompanists.

Tell us something about your latest publication, please?

In Search of Mary Shelley: the girl who wrote Frankenstein was commissioned by Profile for the 200 years of *Frankenstein*. I was incredibly lucky that they came to me. I'd prepared an edition, with Introduction, of Percy Bysshe Shelley for Fabers a couple of years earlier: they read this, and – bingo. Most of the best things in my working life have been like this: unexpected. I loved writing the biography and tried to make it extremely readable story-telling; but it is scrupulously researched, and I did make some original discoveries. I tidied these all away to the dozens of pages of notes at the back of the book. I didn't want the confetti of superscript footnote numbers. I think it stops the reading flow! I wanted to write a sort of psychological biography – to find the person behind the facts – but not to fictionalise. Nothing is invented or speculative: where I speculate I do so out loud. I start each chapter with a freeze-frame image, then let the people in it move. It's lovely writing in a genre that's so widely read, and also lovely that I seem to be writing lots of supplementary things about Mary Shelley still: articles and essays and talks. This allows me to explore some of the things I didn't have room for in the book. *In Search of Mary Shelley* has had a wonderful critical reception – I'm so grateful – as well as being serialised on BBC R4 (not that I did the abridgement), etc. It's almost like Frankenstein's monster – it's grown away from me!

Can writing be taught?

There's a ton of craft in writing, and that requires an apprenticeship – Malcom Gladwell's 10,000 hours of practice, perhaps – just like any other craft. Gift can't be taught, but it can be suffocated or released by opportunity and circumstance. In 'the old days', writers (who for this reason alone were usually male) had a Classical education. They were making poems and practising rhetoric (through translating the Classics) from when they were six, seven years old.

They also had enormously gifted teachers – in a very few, rarified schools and universities – who mentored them informally through patronage and, to put it another way, nepotism. I don't think that's good enough. I think if we want the best and the hungriest writers, they won't just come from that narrow stratum of society.

Have you given or attended creative writing workshops and if you have, share your experiences a bit, please?

I've given so many, in community settings and to kids and adults and students – where to start? I'm now Professor of Poetry and Director of the Poetry Centre at the University of Roehampton in London. It's a half-time Chair so that I have time to write.

I try to bring my experiences as a violinist to bear when I workshop. I was taught by some amazing musicians, and what made them great teachers (and people) was that they brought their own practice, and enthusiasms, into the teaching room. It wasn't being taught by a full-time teacher, while the world of actual professional music-making went on somewhere else. It was the world of professional music coming into the teaching room and embracing you. That's the conservatoire system and it's phenomenally inspiring and exciting: and I have to say that its standards are far higher than even Oxbridge (where I went on to do my first degree in my twenties).

Flash fiction – how driven is the popularity of this form by social media like Twitter and its word limits? Do you see Twitter as somehow leading to shorter fiction?

We used to ask the same about SMS messages, and that both did and didn't happen. New media and contexts will always throw up exciting new forms we can do new things with. At the same time many old forms will continue (though maybe they will change shape in ways we can't imagine) because of the things we can do with them – that point about our own capacities and needs as readers and writers is a really important one.

Finally, what question do you wish someone would ask about your writing, and how would you answer it?

I wish, of course, that a publisher, film/radio producer would ask me what I'd like to do next ... It's much nicer making things than it is talking about oneself!

Finally, finally, some Quick Pick Questions:

E-books or print?
Print. E-books don't smell.
Dog or cat?
Both. But not in the same room, obviously.
Reviews – read or don't read?
Read.
Best city to inspire a writer: London, Dublin, New York (Other)?
Belgrade.
Favourite meal out: breakfast, lunch, dinner?
Dinner. It can go on, and on ...
Weekly series or box sets?
Neither.
Favourite colour?
Varies constantly. Today, pearl.
Rolling Stones or Beatles?
Stones.
Night or day?
Dunno!

Artist's Statement

Cover image: *Telling Lies,* encaustic and oil,
by Ann-Marie Brown

Ann-Marie Brown was born in the north of England, and moved with her parents to her father's hometown in Ireland, before emigrating with her family to Canada. She has lived around the world, and currently makes her studio/home on the west coast of Canada with her husband, son, dog, and the occasional bear. Her paintings have been exhibited across Canada and the US, and are included in private, public and corporate collections.

Biographical Details

Liam Aungier has had poems published in *The Irish Times, Poetry Ireland Review, Cyphers* and previously in *Crannóg*. His first book, *Apples in Winter*, was published by Doghouse in 2005.

Colin Bancroft is currently in exile in the wilds of the North Pennines finishing off a PhD on Robert Frost and Nature.

Neil Banks lives in Bray, County Wicklow. His stories and poems have featured in *New Irish Writing, Crannóg 32, The Stinging Fly, The Shot Glass Journal, Burning Bush 2* and on *RTÉ Radio*.

Amanda Bell's publications include *Undercurrents* (Alba Publishing, 2016) which was shortlisted for the Touchstone Distinguished Books Award and placed second in the HSA's Merit Book Award; an illustrated children's book called *The Lost Library Book* (Onslaught, 2017); and *First the Feathers* (Doire Press, 2018) which was shortlisted for the Shine Strong Award. *The Loneliness of the Sasquatch*, translated from an original by Gabriel Rosenstock, will be published by Alba Publishing in November 2018.

Peter Branson, a native of N. Staffordshire, has lived in a village in Cheshire, UK, for the last twenty-seven years. A former teacher and lecturer in English Literature and creative writing and poetry tutor, he is now a full-time poet, songwriter and traditional-style singer whose poetry has been published by journals in Britain, the USA, Canada, Ireland, Australasia and South Africa, including *Acumen, Agenda, Ambit, Anon, Envoi, The London Magazine, The North, Prole, The Warwick Review, Iota, The Butcher's Dog, The Frogmore Papers, The Interpreter's House, SOUTH, Crannóg, THE SHOp, Causeway, Columbia Review, Main Street Rag, Measure and Other Poetry*. His *Selected Poems, Red Hill*, came out in 2013. His latest collection, *Hawk Rising*, from Lapwing, Belfast, was published in April 2016. He has won prizes and been placed in a number of poetry competitions over recent years, including a 'highly commended' in the Petra Kenny International, first prizes in the Grace Dieu and the Envoi International and a special commendation in the Wigtown. He was shortlisted for the most recent Poetry Business Pamphlet and Collection competition.

Paul Bregazzi's poetry has appeared widely in print and online in Ireland, the UK, France, Mexico and the US. His work has been shortlisted and awarded in numerous competitions in Europe and the US, including the Bridport Prize. He was Cúirt New Writer of the Year, 2017.

Rachel Burns has had poetry published in literary magazines such as *The Lake, South, Mslexia, Head Stuff, South Bank Poetry, Ambit*, and *The Herald* newspaper. Her poems have been anthologised in *#MeToo, Poems for Grenfell Tower*, and *Please Hear What I'm Not Saying*.

Maeve Casey grew up in Limerick, qualified as a psychologist and worked at the Social Psychology Research Unit and the Women's Studies Centre at University College Dublin. Her short stories have been published in New Irish Writing and broadcast on RTÉ Radio 1 and BBC Radio 4. Her novel, *Tribal Gods*, has been published recently by Wordsonthestreet.

Sandra Coffey is a writer from Galway. She has been published in journals in Ireland and the UK including *Crannóg, Honest Ulsterman, Incubator Magazine,* and *Silver Apples*. She was previously shortlisted for the Irish Short Story of the Year. One of her stories was chosen for an anthology published by RTÉ, Ballpoint Press and the *Farmer's Journal*. She is working on her first short story collection and tweets @SandraCoffey.

Louise G Cole won the Hennessy Award for Emerging Poetry in March 2018, and has been selected by the UK Poet Laureate Carol Ann Duffy for publication in a pamphlet in the Laureate's Choice series in February 2019. She is a member of the committee of Strokestown International Poetry Festival. She performs monthly at the Word Corner Café in Carrick-on-Shannon, and blogs at https://louisegcolewriter.wordpress.com.

Sinéad Creedon is a recent graduate of English Literature studies from Trinity College Dublin. She has been published in *Ireland's Zine* and *The Attic*. Her blog is www.sonderful.wordpress.com.

Emily Cullen is author of two poetry collections, *In Between Angels and Animals* (Arlen House, 2013) and *No Vague Utopia* (Ainnir Publishing, 2003). Her third book of poems, *Conditional Perfect*, will be published by Doire Press in 2019. She is Programme Director of Galway's annual Cúirt International Festival of Literature.

Barbara De Franceschi is an Australian poet. Besides three collections of poetry, her work has been published widely in Australia, in other countries, online and featured on national and regional radio. She has served as artist-in-residence for the University Department of Rural Health as part of the *Art in Health* programme, an initiative to enhance communication for health science students.

Theodore Deppe is the author of six volumes of poetry, most recently *Liminal Blue* (Arlen House, 2016).

Mairéad Donnellan's work has been published in various magazines and anthologies. She has been shortlisted in national poetry competitions including Cúirt new writing prize, North West words competition and Doire Press chapbook competition. Her poetry has been broadcast on RTÉ radio. She was winner of the Ledwidge poetry prize in 2013 and the Trócaire/Poetry Ireland prize in 2016. Two of her poems featured in the Irish Times Hennessy New Irish Writing, 2018. She received the Tyrone Guthrie Award from Cavan Arts Office this year.

Chinua Ezenwa-Ohaeto has won the Association of Nigerian Authors Literary Award for the ANA/Mazariyya Teen Author Prize (poetry), 2009 and the Speak to the Heart

Inc. Poetry Competition, 2016. He was a runner-up in the Etisalat Prize for Literature, Flash fiction, 2014. He won the Castello di Duino Poesia Prize for an unpublished poem, 2018. His work has appeared in *Lunaris Review, AFREADA, Kalahari Review, Praxis magazine,* and *Elsewhere.*

Ewa Fornal is a visual artist from Poland living in Dublin. She graduated from the Academy of Fine Arts in Poznan, Poland in 2007. She moved to Dublin in 2009 and has exhibited widely in group exhibitions in Ireland and abroad including at Filmbase Temple Bar, The Ivy House, Drumcondra, The Crow Gallery, Temple Bar, Festival of World Cultures, Dún Laoghaire, Monster Truck Gallery, Temple Bar, Garter Lane Arts Centre, Box Heart Gallery in Pittsburgh, Pennsylvania. She is a self-published children's books author and illustrator.

Rebecca Gethin has had two pamphlets published in 2017: *A Sprig of Rowan* by Three Drops Press and *All the Time in the World* by Cinnamon Press who also published an earlier collection and two novels. She has been a Hawthornden Fellow. In 2018 she jointly won the Coast to Coast Pamphlet competition and has received a writing residency at Brisons Veor. www.rebeccagethin.wordpress.com

Angela Graham is an Irish writer living in Wales. She completed her short story collection, *A City Burning* in 2017 with the support of a bursary from Literature Wales and is working on a novel set in rural Northern Ireland backed by a grant from the Arts Council there. She was a finalist in the Rhys Davies Short Story Competition and has published in *The Honest Ulsterman, The Lonely Crowd* and other journals. She is an award-winning TV and film producer. Her story was completed during the term of a Literature Wales Writer's bursary supported by The National Lottery through the Arts Council of Wales.

Kevin Griffin has had poems published in *Crannóg, THE SHOp, Revival, Boyne Berries, Riposte, Stony Thursday Book, Labour of Love, Salzburg Review, Orbis, North West Words* and *Pennine Ink.*

Richard W Halperin's most recent collections are *Catch Me While You Have the Light* (Salmon), *Three Poem Sequences* (Lapwing), and *Tea in Tbilis*i (Lapwing), all 2018.

Kevin Higgins is co-organiser of Over The Edge literary events in Galway, Ireland. He teaches poetry workshops at Galway Arts Centre, Creative Writing at Galway Technical Institute, and is Creative Writing Director for the National University of Ireland's Galway Summer School. He is poetry critic of *The Galway Advertiser.* His poetry is discussed in *The Cambridge Introduction to Modern Irish Poetry* and features in the generation-defining anthology *Identity Parade: new British and Irish poets* (ed. Roddy Lumsden, Bloodaxe, 2010) and in *The Hundred Years' War: modern war poems* (ed. Neil Astley, Bloodaxe, April 2014). His poetry has been translated into Greek, Spanish, Italian, Japanese, Serbian, Russian, and Portuguese. In 2014 his poetry was the subject of a paper *The Case of Kevin Higgins, or, The Present State of Irish Poetic Satire* presented by David Wheatley at a Symposium on Satire at the University of Aberdeen.

2016 – The Selected Satires of Kevin Higgins was published by NuaScéalta in 2016; a pamphlet of political poems *The Minister For Poetry Has Decreed* was published, also in 2016, by the Culture Matters imprint of the UK-based Manifesto Press. His poems have been quoted in *The Daily Telegraph, The Times* (UK), *The Independent, The Daily Mirror*, and on *Tonight With Vincent Browne*. He has published five collections of poetry with Salmon, most recently *Song of Songs 2.0: New & Selected Poems* (2017).

Rosa Jones has had poetry and personal essays published in a variety of print and online publications since 2015. She is one third of Not4U Collective, which runs safe and inclusive feminist nights in Dublin for emerging writers and artists.

Marina Kazakova is a Communications Officer at Victim Support Europe. She has an MA in Public Relations and Transmedia. She is working on her practice-based PhD in Arts: *Lyric Film-Poem: a research on how the unique characteristics of lyric poetry can be expressed in film* at Luca School of Arts, KU Leuven.

Seán Kenny is the winner of a Hennessy Literary Award and was named Over The Edge New Writer of the Year. His stories have appeared in Over the Edge and Hennessy anthologies, *Banshee, Crannóg, The Irish Times, The Incubator* and *Southword* in addition to being broadcast on RTÉ Radio 1.

Pippa Little's first full collection *Overwintering* was published by Carcanet in 2012 and was shortlisted for The Seamus Heaney Centre Award. Her second collection, *Twist,* published by Arc in 2017, was shortlisted for The Saltire Society's Poetry Book of the Year. Her work appears widely in print, online and in anthologies. She is Scots and lives in Northumberland where she is a Royal Literary Fund Fellow at Newcastle University.

Paul McCarrick has had poetry published in *Boyne Berries, Skylight 47, Bangor Literary Journal,* and *The Stinging Fly.* His novel was longlisted in the 2014 Irish Writers' Centre Novel Fair Competition. His poetry was placed 3rd in the 2015 Over The Edge New Writer Competition and was longlisted in 2016.

Una Mannion is a teacher and writer living in County Sligo. In 2017, she was awarded the Hennessy prize for Emerging Poetry and was the winner of the Doolin Short Story, Cúirt International Short Story and Allingham Short Fiction prizes. She has been published in *The Lonely Crowd, Ambit, Bare Fiction, The Irish Times* and has won numerous other prizes for her poetry and fiction.

Carol McGill has had work published in the anthology *Words To Tie To Bricks* as well as in the online magazines *Rookie* and *Germ.* Her short stories have also been published in *Silver Apples Magazine* and *Number Eleven Magazine.* She has been shortlisted and longlisted in the Brilliant Flash Fiction writing competition, and in 2015 she won the Puffin/RTÉ Guide teen writing competition in Ireland.

Mari Maxwell received The Story House Ireland's inaugural residency and participated in the Irish Writers Centre XBorders programme in 2017. She tweets at @MariMaxwell17 and blogs at https://lineatatime.wordpress.com.

Patrick Moran's poetry was shortlisted for the Hennessy Award in 1990. His poems are widely published in Ireland and the UK, and feature in many anthologies, including *Windharp: Poems of Ireland Since 1916* and *Even the Daybreak: 35 Years of Salmon Poetry*. His prose and poetry has featured on the RTÉ radio programme *Sunday Miscellany*. He has published three poetry collections: *The Stubble Fields* (Dedalus, 2001), *Green* (Salmon, 2008) and *Bearings* (Salmon, 2015). His next collection, *LIFELINES*, is due in spring 2019.

Ciarán Ó Gríofa grew up in east County Clare and lives in Limerick City. He is a member of the Limerick Writers' Centre writing group.

Christine Pacyk's work has been published in *Jet Fuel Review, Beloit Poetry Journal, Crannóg*, and *Zone 3*, among other journals. Collaborative poems written with Virginia Smith Rice appear in *Jet Fuel Review*, and in *They Said: A Multi-Genre Anthology of Contemporary Collaborative Writing* (Black Lawrence Press, 2018). She holds an MFA in poetry from Northwestern University.

Nome Emeka Patrick is a Nigerian artist who writes from a room close to banana trees and bird songs. His works are on or forthcoming on *gaze, Vagabond City, Prachya review, Tuck Magazine, African Writer, Kalahari Review, Dwarts*, and others. He is a student of English language and literature in the University of Benin, Nigeria.

Ruth Quinlan won the 2018 Galway University Hospital Arts Trust – Poems for Patience competition, the 2014 Over the Edge New Writer of the Year Award and the 2012 Hennessy Literary Award for First Fiction. She has also been shortlisted or runner-up for other competitions like Cúirt New Writing, Francis Ledwidge Poetry Awards, and Doolin Writers' Weekend. Her work has been published in such outlets as the *Irish Independent, Crannóg, Skylight 47*, and has been nominated for the Forward Poetry Prize.

Jess Raymon is a writer living in Dublin.

stephanie roberts is a 2018 Pushcart Prize nominee and a Silver Needle Press winner for Poem of the Week. Her work has been previously featured in *Crannóg*, as well as *Banshee, Arcturus, The Stockholm Review of Literature, Atlanta Review, Burning House Press, Occulum*, and elsewhere.

Clare Sawtell's first collection, *The Next Dance* (Wordsonthestreet) was published in 2014. Her most recent collection, *Soft Notes and Departures* (Lapwing) was published in December 2017. Her poems have been published in *Crannóg, THE SHOp, The Stony Thursday Book, Earthlines* and *The Clare Champion*.

Knute Skinner's collected poems, *Fifty Years: Poems 1957–2007*, was published by Salmon Poetry in 2007. A limited edition of his poems, translated into Italian by Roberto Nassi, appeared from Damocle Edizioni, Chioggia, Italy. His most recent collections are *Concerned Attentions* (Salmon, 2013), *Against All Odds* (Lapwing Publications, 2016) and *The Life That I Have* (Salmon, 2018).

Keshia Starrett's work has appeared in various magazines and anthologies; most recently *The Interpreter's House, The Honest Ulsterman*, and *Ink, Sweat & Tears*. Her poetry pamphlet, *Hysterical*, is available from Burning Eye Books. She has an MA in Creative Writing from the University of Manchester and is currently a PhD student at Leeds Beckett University.

Jamie Stedmond is currently completing an MA in Creative Writing at UCD. His poems have recently appeared, or are forthcoming, in *Abridged, The Honest Ulsterman, The Stony Thursday Book, Headstuff.org* and *Porridge Magazine*.

Jill Talbot's writing has appeared in *Geist, Rattle, Poetry Is Dead, The Puritan, Matrix, subTerrain, The Tishman Review, The Cardiff Review, PRISM, Southword, The Stinging Fly*, and others. She won the PRISM Grouse Grind Lit Prize. She was shortlisted for the Matrix Lit POP Award for fiction and the Malahat Far Horizons Award for poetry. She lives on Gabriola Island, BC.

Christine Valters Paintner's poems have been published in several journals including *Galway Review, Boyne Berries, The Stinging Fly, Skylight 47, Crannóg*, and *North West Words*. Her first collection, *Dreaming of Stones*, will be published by Paraclete Press in 2019. You can find more at AbbeyoftheArts.com.

Hannah van Didden has been published in *Southerly, Hippocampus Magazine, Breach, Atticus Review, Southword*, and *thirtyseven*.

Karla Van Vliet is the author of two collections of poems, *From the Book of Remembrance*, and *The River From My Mouth*. She is an Edna St Vincent Millay Poetry Prize finalist, and a two-time Pushcart and Best of the Net nominee. Her poems have appeared in *Acumen, Poet Lore, The Tishman Review, Green Mountains Review, Crannóg* and others. Her chapbook *Fragments: From the Lost Book of the Bird Spirit* is forthcoming from Folded Word. She is a co-founder and editor of *deLuge Journal*. She is an Integrative Dreamwork analyst, artist and administrator of the New England Young Writers' Conference at Bread Loaf, Middlebury College.

Kim Whysall-Hammond is a writer from the UK.

Stay in touch with
Crannóg

www.crannogmagazine.com

Lightning Source UK Ltd.
Milton Keynes UK
UKHW02f0614081018
330076UK00003B/70/P